The Dangerous Christmas Ornament

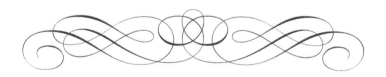

BOB SIEGEL

Preface

This book is purely fiction, a fantasy story from start to finish. It is not my intention to teach any new theology or belief about God, angels or the supernatural.

Contents

Chapter One

Aunt Loureen

Year : 1999

Dad didn't like the present. I guess that's where my story begins. Dad didn't like the present. He didn't like it at all. He said it annoyed him. Most of my friends were confused. They couldn't see why a gift should annoy anybody, especially a gift as small as a simple Christmas ornament. To me it wasn't so unusual. I don't mean that I understood Dad's problem with the gift. It's just that I didn't understand any of the reasons Dad got annoyed, and he got annoyed so much I was used to it.

He got annoyed when kids played in our front yard. He got annoyed when people called to sell him something over the phone. Actually, he got annoyed whenever the phone rang whether people were trying to sell him something or not. He got annoyed when there were too many bills in the mail or too many commercials on TV. He got very annoyed with people at his office, and he talked about them everyday when he returned home from work. What annoyed him most of all was Mom telling him that he got too annoyed. Sometimes he got so annoyed that he yelled and made my little sister cry. But then he would explain that he wasn't really yelling and we would all feel better.

Anyway, today Dad was annoyed at the ornament. The ornament was a present from my Aunt Loureen. She was Dad's sister, and she spent every Christmas with us because she didn't have a husband or kids of her own. Aunt Loureen is my favorite aunt, which is only fair because she always says I'm her favorite nephew. Dad always looked forward to her coming, but then they argued the whole time she was here. Adults are hard to figure out sometimes. Still, I enjoyed Aunt Loureen's visits because she usually acted a lot different from other adults. She liked the kinds of things that kids liked. She liked snowball fights. She liked *Twister*. She even liked candy, and she shared her candy without always reminding us of all the cavities we could get. Mostly, she liked Christmas. I liked Christmas too and I couldn't imagine a Christmas without Aunt Loureen. The presents and cards and decorations were already fun, but Aunt Loureen added so much more. She used to tell us that during Christmas, "God moved heaven just a little bit closer to Earth."

My parents also looked forward to Christmas but not the way Aunt Loureen did. She always arrived one week before with a suitcase full of extra tinsel for our tree. After redecorating the entire house, she took over the kitchen and baked six different kinds of pies. She also helped Mom with the turkey and junk. But that wasn't all. She gave three presents apiece to each member of my family, one on Christmas Eve and the rest Christmas morning. Nobody was allowed to open anything until Aunt Loureen read the Christmas story out loud. "Both versions," she would remind us, "from *Matthew* as well as *Luke*." Aunt Loureen always stayed till a few days after New Year's and took my sister and me out driving to see if any Christmas lights were still up in the neighborhood because Aunt Loureen knew that Christmas wasn't really over till the last light came down from the last house. Even then, she went on celebrating Christmas herself till March. The way she put it; "If you're going to have winter, you may as well have Christmas along with it."

Aunt Loureen was in her forties like Dad, but she looked much younger. Dad was partly bald and mostly gray. He was also a little bit fat. But Aunt Loureen was thin and she had long dark hair. Mom was sure she dyed it but she could never find a bottle of hair dye when Aunt Loureen visited. Mom did bleach her own hair to make herself look blonde. I think she figured any other woman her age must be doing the same thing. Mom also dieted but she wasn't as thin as Aunt Loureen. Only one thing about Aunt Loureen did look kind of old; her long dresses. Her dresses made her look like a visitor from the olden days. And her voice sounded very proper, like the way somebody from England talks, except that Aunt Loureen wasn't from England. She did visit England a lot but she wasn't *from* England.

Christmas this year had been really cool so far. I was in the sixth grade now so my presents were less like toys and more like the kinds of things an older kid would want, except for clothes. Clothes were always boring presents no matter how old I was and yeah, I did get the usual stack of clothes again from Mom, but Mom and Dad together also got me a box of my own tools, so it kind of made up for all the socks and underwear and stuff. Aunt Loureen gave me a sweater, a computer game, and the book *Tom Sawyer*. Aunt Loureen was concerned that I didn't read enough of the classics, so she always saw to it that one of my three gifts was some kind of book. "Computers are fine," she would tell me. "I'm all for progress, but we must never stop reading books."

The room smelled of pine needles from the tree and Aunt Loureen's strong perfume. I never asked what brand it was, but whenever I smell that perfume, I think of Christmas time. I was filled with turkey, stuffing, mashed potatoes and gravy, cranberry sauce and Aunt Loureen's special chocolate pie with whipped cream. *The First Noel* was playing on our stereo. I was starting to sing to it when Aunt Loureen announced that she had another present, one for the whole family.

It came in a very small box. She allowed me to pull the red ribbon and gold wrapping paper off. Inside was the gnarliest Christmas ornament I had ever seen. It was made of thin glass and shaped like a ball. Inside the ball was a cool looking pink castle surrounded by a blue moat. It also had that snow stuff which fell inside the glass when you turned it upside down.

"Is that a make believe castle or a real place?" my sister Shelly asked.

"The castle belongs to King Crescent who once ruled the country of Lumas for over 20 years."

"Lumas?" I asked. "Where's that?" I reached for the family globe.

"Put the globe down, Sonny. You won't find this country on any map."

"Why doesn't that surprise me?" Dad muttered.

"Did you say something, James?" Aunt Loureen asked suspiciously.

"Yes...Ah...I said, 'Thanks for the gift.' I know just where to hang it."

"Before you do, there's something about the ornament you should know. All of you! Now pay attention. Sit down, Sonny! You especially need to hear this."

"OK," Dad said. "We're all sitting. We're all listening."

"This is no ordinary Christmas ornament."

"Oh?" Dad looked like he was ready for another one of their arguments.

"The ornament has a charm attached to it."

3

My sister got very excited and ran toward the ornament. Shelly was only six, so she got excited easily.

"A charm," Dad repeated, staring at the floor, not looking nearly as excited as Shelly.

"Yes, James. A special charm."

"A special charm. I see...Well...If it's going to have a charm, it might as well be special."

Dad seemed bothered, like he had expected Aunt Loureen to make such comments about simple things like Christmas ornaments. But I loved these surprises. "What kind of charm, Aunt Loureen?"

"I can't really say, Sonny. All I know is that this ornament will bless the family who owns it."

"How? How will it bless us?"

She shrugged. "Only time will tell."

"Thanks, Loureen," Mom said politely. "It's lovely."

"I still don't understand, Aunt Loureen. I wanna know more about this charm."

"I don't blame you, Sonny, but that's all I can say. You know what I know. We'll have to be patient."

Oh. I almost forgot to tell you. Aunt Loureen always called me *Sonny*, even though my name is Mike. And she called Dad *James* even though Mom called him *Jim*.

Dad bounced the ornament lightly and caught it with his hand. "If you don't know what the charm is, then how do you know it has one?"

"The fellow who sold it to me said so."

"Oh... Well. You didn't explain it like that. Some salesman said it has a charm. OK. That's good enough for me!"

"Jim." Mom put her hand gently on Dad's shoulder.

"No, Marian, I have to do this. Look, Loureen. It's a nice present but I'd just as soon you not attach stories to it."

"I didn't attach anything, Brother. The ornament came as it is."

"The ornament is pretty, and we'll hang it on the tree. That's all."

"But that's not all. There's more."

"No. There is *not* more."

"Now, James, really. What kind of gift would a mere ornament be? Obviously there's something special about it, or I would have bought you something else."

"Loureen..." Dad, stopped himself and calmed down a bit. He didn't like to yell as loud when his sister was around. That's another reason why I liked her. "OK, OK. Fine...It has a special charm. But since you don't know what the charm is, there's no point in talking about it, is there?"

"On the contrary, that makes talking all the more fun."

Dad just sat there frowning.

"My poor brother. Don't you have any imagination at all? Don't you enjoy mystery? The anticipation is everything."

"Do me a favor. Next time just bring us a basket of fruit."

"Jim," Mom said. "You're being rude. Loureen was kind enough to bring us a delightful Christmas present, and we are all thankful. Aren't we children?"

"Sure," I said. "It's cool!"

"I love it!" Shelly shouted.

"Jim?"

"Thanks, Loureen. It's nice."

"Jim?"

"It's *very* nice."

Chapter Two

Ornament Rules and Lima Beans

Later that day, the whole family played a new board game that Aunt Loureen brought with her. I don't remember what it was called, but it was fun and it had those cards you draw with questions that helped you move further on the board if you could answer the question correctly. Aunt Loureen said it was important for families to play indoor board games together on Christmas, something about it being an "intimate thing to do." Aunt Loureen usually won when the game tested our knowledge. That's probably because she worked as a school teacher. She seemed to know a little about every subject. She was as good at science as she was at history. A lot of times, after she got an answer right, she'd go on and offer more information about the question till Dad told her to stop and get on with her next turn.

I'm not sure where Aunt Loureen got all her facts because she knew some things that weren't written in books or taught in school, at least, not at my school.

Today she was going on and on about cats because one of the questions asked about some strange animal in the feline family. Aunt Loureen started to explain how she had discovered years ago that cats can not only talk but are smart about practically everything. While arguing the point, Dad said, "Then how come nobody ever hears them talk if they're so intelligent?" He pointed to Caligula, our fluffy black and white cat who was stretched out comfortably over Mom's best sofa. "That fat, furry, blob hardly moves, let alone speak. If he died, it would be a week before anyone even noticed."

"It's precisely because they *are* intelligent that they *don't* talk," Aunt Loureen carefully explained. "Cats are shrewd enough to know that if their aptitude were ever discovered, people would put them to work."

"Loureen? What goes on inside that head?"

"Oh honestly, James! Calm down for a minute and you'll see the logic."

"Logic? Why, dear sister, you are allergic to logic. Logic runs from the sight of you."

"But this is very logical. Why should a cat work when he can have three hearty meals a day and the run of the house for free?"

"Ah," Dad teased. "So what you're saying is that cats are Democrats."

I don't know what they said after that because I always stop listening when adults talk about Democrats or Republicans or stuff like that.

❄ ❄ ❄

"You're fascinated with the ornament, aren't you? You can't seem to take your eyes off of it."

It was late at night. I was sitting by the fireplace, drinking a mug of hot chocolate I had micro waved for myself. I thought I was the last one up, and Aunt Loureen scared me with her loud, sudden question.

"Yeah, Aunt Loureen. I really like it a lot. There's something about that castle."

She smiled, almost like she was proud of me for liking it. Then she pulled the ornament off the tree and held it up against the light from the fire. "Oh yes. Reflected in this glass are many stories...many adventures."

"I'd love to know what some of them are. I sure wish you knew more about that charm."

"Actually...Come over here, Sonny."

"You know! You *do* know how it works!"

With a sneaky smile, she nodded her head.

"But why didn't you tell us before?"

"It was meant that I should tell only you."

"Tell me, Aunt Loureen!"

"Settle down!"

"But I..."

"Settle down or I won't tell you anything! OK...Now, first of all, this is a secret. Understand?"

"Sure. Sure...Cross my heart!"

"Very well. I have your promise." Aunt Loureen looked very concerned, like she was about to tell me the most important thing in the world. She stopped talking for a second or so. Then she whispered. "You've heard the story of Aladdin's magic lamp?"

"Well, yeah. Everybody has. But that's only a fairy tale. There's no such thing as magic."

"No such thing as magic...And just exactly how do you know that? Hmm? That father of yours. He has sadly neglected a key part of your education."

"So...I'm gonna get three wishes? Is that it?"

"You get wishes, yes. But forget about that 'three' nonsense. That part *is* a fairy tale."

"How many wishes *do* I get?"

"It's unlimited."

"Unlimited?"

"Wait...Just hold on...Let me explain...Unlimited so long as Christmas season is still here."

"But it's Christmas Day already. How long will Christmas season stay?"

"Until the last light comes off of the last house. Really, Sonny...Haven't I taught you already?"

"I can wish for anything? Anything at all? So long as Christmas lights are still up? We'll just leave ours out all year long."

"Ha! Good luck talking your father into that. No, the wishes will eventually stop. But let's not get ahead of ourselves. Let's live in the present. I must explain to you how this works."

"I know! I rub it!"

"Rub it…Oh, my word…Hollywood. No, you don't have to rub it. You don't even have to hold it. All you have to do is be in the same room."

"Wow!"

"But there's a catch, a very important catch. First of all, the ornament works only within reason."

"I don't understand."

"I mean you can't just ask for anything. The ornament has a mind of its own as well an ornament should. You can't ask it to send you to Mars or to make you President of the United States."

"I wasn't gonna ask for those things."

"Neither can you ask for all the gold in the world or for the ability to fly."

Now I was disappointed. "Well, then what *can* it do?"

"Anything within reason. You'll see when you start making wishes."

"OK, I wish for…"

"Just a minute…There are more provisions."

"I knew this was too good to be true."

"Sonny, anything that is really good is always true. But there is one more very important stipulation."

"What's a stipulation?"

"A condition…When you wish for something good and when the wish is granted, something bad also happens."

"Huh?"

"At the time you get your wish, something bad happens along with it."

"You're scaring me, Aunt Loureen."

"I'm being honest. You're a big twelve year old boy. You're in the sixth grade. You're becoming a young man. I remember saying that to myself on your last birthday. I think you can deal with this kind of responsibility."

"Why should I make a wish if something bad is gonna happen?"

"It won't happen to you. It'll happen to someone near you, somebody else in the same room."

"Oh…Oh…That's different. But I'll still get what I wish for?"

"Yes."

"I guess that's OK."

"You guess? No concern for others so long as you get your own wish?"

"Well, you gave it to me. Don't you want me to use it?"

"I want you to use it, yes. But it has tremendous power, and it must be used responsibly."

"What kinds of bad things can it do? Would it make somebody sick or make them die?"

"Probably nothing that bad, at least not as a general rule."

"Well, what then?"

"I'll give you an example. Earlier when I said I didn't know the charm, that was true. I was not just pretending to keep it a secret for you. I meant exactly what I said. *I did not know*."

"But..."

"Shh! Hush! Let me finish. You're about to ask me how I know now all of a sudden. Because, my dear nephew, you already made your first wish without realizing it. A moment ago, you said, and I quote, 'I sure wish you knew more about that charm.'"

"You mean...? Wow!"

"You wished and all at once I knew. Don't ask me how. It wasn't as though I figured anything out. No ideas instantly popped into my head. Instead, I felt as if I had already known for years and was now remembering again."

"That's so cool."

"Cool, eh? Don't you want to know what the bad thing is? After all, it happened to me because I was the only one in the room with you."

"You look the same. I don't see anything bad."

"Bad things are seldom obvious, Sonny. The bad thing is that it made me a liar to the rest of your family. They think I knew nothing about the ornament because that's what I told them."

"Oh that's no big deal. Dad doesn't believe in the charm anyway."

"It still made me a liar. I don't like being a liar."

"It wasn't a lie when you said it."

"Doesn't matter. It's a lie now. So anyway, now you've seen an example."

"I don't really think that's so bad, Aunt Loureen."

"Oh, you don't, eh?"

I got up and started walking away.

"What are you doing now? You look like you're getting ready to pout."

"Well you gave me this great gift, but now you act like you're mad at me for wanting to use it."

"Sonny, stop that pouting. Stop it right now!"

We always had leftovers the night after Christmas. The turkey and stuffing was still good, but Mom made some lima beans to go with it, and I hated lima beans. At first it looked like I was gonna get away with not eating them because nobody seemed to notice. But then my little brat sister, Shelly, ruined everything.

"Daddy, Mike isn't eating his lima beans."

"Shut up and mind your own business!"

"Michael," Mom said, "I will not have the words *shut up* in this house."

"You know what you are?" I said to Shelly. "You're a fink!"

Shelly stuck her tongue out at me from across the table. I wanted to run over and pull every curl out of her blonde little head. I'm not usually a brother who would hurt his sister, but she was making me very angry. Anyway, it didn't matter. In front of our parents I couldn't do much more than sit still and take what comes.

"Eat your lima beans," Dad said. "They're good for you."

I could never understand why parents told kids about food being good for them. They seemed to think that this was some kind of fantastic new piece of information which would instantly change our minds and cause us to actually enjoy eating whatever it was we didn't wanna eat. I know many kids, and I've never seen this work on any of them. But for some reason, parents still like saying it every single time.

"I think I'm allergic to lima beans."

"Nice try," Dad said. "Now eat them, and don't make me tell you again."

Mom spoke more gently. "Honey, you were tested for allergies. And you are not allergic to lima beans."

"I think I am. I think that's why I don't like them. And once I threw up after eating them."

"Are you going to stop fussing?" Dad shouted. "Or do I have to come over and feed you myself? In this family we finish our plates!"

Aunt Loureen came to my rescue. "Oh James, why carry on so? If he doesn't like it, why make him eat it?"

"This doesn't concern you, Loureen."

"It most certainly does. I'm sitting at the same table as the rest of you, and I have to listen to you bellyache."

"He's my son, and I want him to eat his lima beans. He needs the vitamins."

"So I'll give him a vitamin tablet after dinner."

"Butt out, Loureen!"

"Oh Gooseburgers! Butt out yourself."

"So help me..." Dad looked like he was about to shout, but instead, he paused and lowered his voice. "Now look. If you had kids of your own you'd want them to be healthy."

"I *do* want them to be healthy."

"Yeah? Well good then. Lima beans are healthy."

"Of course they are. But is it worth ruining the kid's dinner? Let him enjoy himself. After all, it's Christmas."

"Christmas was yesterday."

"It's the season, James, the season. Today is still Christmas."

"Oh it's Christmas. Well Whoopty Do Da Day...Let's not eat healthy today. It's Christmas. While we're at it, let's not eat healthy on New Year's Day either or Valentine's Day...And let's not forget Groundhog Day."

"Oh Gooseburgers!"

I've never had a gooseburger. I don't think Aunt Loureen has either. They probably don't even exist. But she said the word a lot.

"Son," my dad continued, "You are going to eat those lima beans. That is just the way it is going to be."

"But I did eat them, Dad."

"All right, now I've had enough of this nonsense." He got up from his seat and came over to my side of the table.

"Honest, Dad! I ate them!"

Mom pointed to my plate. "He's telling the truth, Jim."

Dad looked like he was ready to fall over, for sure enough, there wasn't one lima bean to be found. While he and Aunt Loureen were arguing, I suddenly remembered that since the dining room was attached to the living room where the ornament hung on our tree, I could quietly whisper a wish. It was my very first wish, at least, the very first wish where I actually knew I was wishing. Up till now, I hadn't been too sure about everything Aunt Loureen explained the night before. Today the whole family had driven up to an ice capped mountain and played in the snow all day long, so there wasn't a lot of time to think about the ornament. But I hated lima beans so much, I just had to make the wish. I didn't even have time to wonder what bad thing might happen because to me nothing bad could possibly be worse than an ugly, slimy lima bean. When it worked and I actually saw those horrible beans disappear off my plate, I wanted to jump out of my chair and scream, "It works! Oh Aunt Loureen! Isn't this wonderful? It actually works!" But I knew I would be in big trouble if Dad wasn't somehow convinced that I had actually eaten the things myself, so I pretended as best I could to be calm.

"What's going on here? You could not possibly have eaten them so fast."

"Well, I only had a few left," I lied. "Shelly was the one making a big deal out of it. While you were talking to Aunt Loureen, I finished them."

"You finished them. I'll just bet you did. I thought I saw more than a few."

"But you were sitting way over on the other side. It must have looked like more from over there."

"Yeah? Well let's just check your napkin."

When I was little, I used to stuff my napkin with lima beans, but I hardly ever got away with it. While Dad looked around my plate and under the table I started wondering about the bad thing. It was gonna happen to somebody else, but who? And then I saw them, a little pile of lima beans stacked neatly on Shelly's plate. Nobody had noticed yet, not even Shelly. I tried very hard not to laugh.

Dad scratched his head. "I guess he ate them."

"Can we finish our dinner now in peace?" Mom pleaded.

"Hey Dad, aren't you gonna make Shelly finish *her* beans?"

"I did finish my...Hey!"

Aunt Loureen gave me a sharp glance as she quickly pieced together what had happened. I hoped she wouldn't tell on me. I didn't think she would because, like I said before, Aunt Loureen was different from other adults.

"Your turn, Shelly," Dad said. "Eat your lima beans."

"I did eat them, Daddy."

"What do you call that?"

"Those aren't mine! Those are Mike's! He put them on my plate!"

"How could I do that, Dopey? I've been sitting here the whole time."

"Now, honey," Mom said. "You know Mike didn't put them on your plate."

"Yes he did. This is a trick!"

Lucky for me Dad didn't believe in tricks. "Eat your lima beans, Shelly. I won't tell you again."

"Hey Dad, since I'm done, can I be excused?"

"Yeah sure," he said, still looking confused.

Shelly started crying as I walked away. I ran down the hall as fast as I could, darted into my room, jumped on the bed and started laughing harder than I had ever laughed in my life.

Chapter Three

Caligula, the Family Cat

Just like before, Aunt Loureen and I were the only ones who had not gone to bed. I kind of expected this. She wanted to discuss the incident with Shelly. That's what she called it, "an incident." She didn't yell at me. Aunt Loureen never yelled. She scolded me as much as Dad, but she never hollered the way he did. Even when she scolded, I was comfortable around her. Unlike my dad, the things Aunt Loureen said always sort of made sense.

"I think she deserved it, Aunt Loureen. It may have been kind of bad but it wasn't *really* bad."

"The relationship between good and bad can sometimes be that way, Sonny. But you must be very careful. When you made that wish, you did it so fast, you didn't stop to think about the consequences of your actions. You never guessed that the ornament would work things out the way it did."

"But how can I ever guess? How do I know what some ornament is gonna do?"

"You will learn in time."

"If the ornament has a mind of its own, won't it just *always* make sure that things turn out OK?"

17

"No, it will not! Often the ornament will allow great suffering as a result of careless words."

"You said it did things with reasons."

"Yes. But it doesn't always share the reasons."

"Why not?"

"That information was not given to me. The ornament is very mysterious. Nobody knows exactly where it came from. But trust me, Nephew, you were lucky this time. You must not count on such luck in the future."

"I wanna try it again, Aunt Loureen. I wanna make another wish. What happened tonight was so much fun."

She gave her sly smile. "And just what would you wish for, Nephew?"

"Well...I've been thinking... About cats...About them being smart like you said. So how about it? How about if I make a wish that Caligula could talk?"

"That's not a valid wish, Sonny. Caligula already can talk, like all cats."

"Well I never hear him."

"I explained why. They don't like to talk."

"OK. So I'll wish that he talks anyway, whether he wants to or not. What do you think? Can I?"

"You're asking me? It isn't my decision. Ask the ornament."

"I still wanna know what you think. And...And maybe you should leave the room before I do it. I don't want anything bad to happen to you."

"I'm certainly glad to see you considering that. However, in this particular case I can already tell you what the bad thing will be. It will happen to Caligula. He will not want to be talking. He will hate every minute of it. That will be the bad thing."

"Hmm..."

"What are you thinking?"

"I'm thinking he's just a cat. Maybe it doesn't matter if a bad thing happens to him. And I'm also thinking that talking is not really a bad thing just because he doesn't wanna do it."

"I see. As I said, you're preaching to the choir over here. There's the cat on the sofa, and there's the ornament hanging on the tree. The choice is yours."

It's not that I didn't like the cat. But he wasn't really my pet. Mom brought him home as a kitten a few years ago, mostly for herself and Shelly. Yeah, I guess I liked him OK, but I didn't really care much about him until Aunt Loureen started telling us how smart he was. I felt scared for a second, but I really wanted to do this. "I wish that Caligula, our family cat can...No...I mean...He can already talk...I wish that he *will*. And, I wish that I can hear him."

Nothing happened. Caligula was still sleeping on the couch. He didn't even move.

"This doesn't work, Aunt Loureen."

"Oh Gooseburgers! Of course it works. It worked with the lima beans, didn't it?"

"But you said the ornament wouldn't give me everything I wish for. So maybe the ornament said 'no.'"

"Maybe. But you must remember, cats are very crafty."

"You mean he's faking? He's pretending to be asleep to throw us off?"

She walked over to the sofa and hovered over Caligula. "I'm not sure. The thought occurred."

"What can I do?"

"If he's now compelled by the ornament to talk against his will, he will probably speak only when asked specific questions."

"So I should go over and ask him something?"

She nodded.

"Caligula! Hey, Caligula! How are you today?"

All at once, his head lifted up and his mouth shot open. "How do you think I am, moron? I'm trying to take a nap!"

"Wow! Did you hear that? Did you hear that, Aunt Loureen?"

"I'm afraid I didn't, Sonny."

"But he spoke! He really did! Honest! How could you not hear him?"

She shrugged.

"Don't you believe me?"

"Settle down. Of course I believe you. I saw his head go up, although I see he's now trying to sleep again. I did hear his cat meow. Nothing else."

"But I didn't hear a meow. I heard actual words. Why didn't we both hear him?"

"I don't know. Probably because you were the one who made the wish. I do seem to recall something in your words about *you specifically* hearing him."

"I didn't mean to be the only one."

"Perhaps not, but the ornament took you at your literal words. Although normally a cat could talk to anybody if it so desired, for some reason, because you made that wish, you evidently are the only one who will hear him."

"OK. I'll just make another wish. That's all. I'll wish that everyone else can hear him too."

At this, Caligula lifted his head again. "Oh man! You're gonna ruin everything!"

"Did you hear that?"

"No," Loureen said. "But that's to be expected. If I didn't hear him the first time, why would I hear him the second time? So don't worry about it and don't wish for everyone to hear him. After all, if you do that, some other bad thing will happen."

"Like what?"

"Who knows? But I can make some wild guesses. For one thing, your dad does not like cats."

"Dad doesn't like anything."

"True. But just imagine how a talking cat might make him feel. We don't need your dad in a worse mood than he's already in. The bad thing may just turn out to be poor Caligula headed for the pound."

"Hey man," Caligula chimed in. "Are you paying attention to this? Listen to the chick. She knows what she's talking about."

"Wow! Caligula...It *is* you. You really can talk!"

"All right. So I can talk. So big deal! Keep it under your hat! Will ya?"

"Oh, Aunt Loureen, he's saying all kinds of funny things, even when I don't ask questions."

"Yes, well, when he wants to talk he will. But when he doesn't, you will have to force him. He will never do it out of the goodness of his heart."

"This is so cool!"

"Can't a cat get any sleep around here? You two have been driving me nuts the last two evenings. So help me, if I hear one more word about that stupid ornament! Take it into the other room. Wish for whatever you want, but just leave me out of it!"

He went back to sleep again or at least did a good job pretending.

"So, whenever I want him to talk, all I have to do is ask him a question and he has to answer me?"

"That's the general idea," Aunt Loureen said.

"Hey Caligula! Caligula...Come on, I know you hear me. Dad says you're lazy. Dad says all you do is sleep all day. How do you feel about that?"

"Lazy am I? Ha! That's a good one! Lazy! And what does he do when he's home besides crash on the couch? The only difference between him and me is that he holds the remote control."

"Oh, Aunt Loureen, I really love this!"

Chapter Four

Complicated Wishing

Mom, Dad and Shelly were taking the ornaments off the tree. Garbage day was tomorrow and Dad wanted to put the Christmas tree out by the trash cans. He said the tree was so dry and brittle that it had become a fire hazard.

"Do we really have to take it down today, Dad? Couldn't we leave it up longer?"

"Christmas is over, Son. I'm afraid your Aunt Loureen has put silly ideas into your head about Christmas going on indefinitely."

Mom explained it more gently. "Michael, your father and I love Christmas just as much as everyone else. But all things end. We had a good holiday and next year we will have it again. As for today, we must face it when Christmas vacation is over."

Aunt Loureen wasn't here to argue with them about taking things down. That's because Dad always put it off till she left and returned to her own home. If Dad had his way, the decorations would have come down sooner, but he knew that if he so much as removed one piece of tinsel while his sister was still in the house, she would give him a lecture on the "true length of Christmas season."

"I'd just as soon spare us the aggravation," he always said.

Aunt Loureen had left two days after New Year's. She said she was going back to her own home first. Then she was gonna fly to England like she did every winter. Aunt Loureen liked being in London around Christmas time 'cause it reminded her of Charles Dickens and stuff like that. The school where she worked took most of their Christmas break from the last week of December till the first few weeks of January. My school was different. We got off around the middle of December and then went back early in January. But anyway, Aunt Loureen didn't need to be back at work for a while, so she always went to England after visiting us. I told her I wished she could stay longer. She said I should be careful what I wished for and that we were both lucky we weren't in the living room near the ornament when I spoke so carelessly.

Before going, she did take Shelly and me out driving around one last time to see how many Christmas lights were up. Some of the houses, maybe about one third of them, still seemed to be celebrating. Aunt Loureen described them as "blinking faithfully like trusted old friends," but I knew that in the weeks ahead I would see a few less each night until the last one was gone. When that time came, the magic ornament wouldn't work any more.

I had never liked saying goodbye to Christmas decorations. I just hated watching the small figures come down from our fireplace mantel. Mom removed everything from the manger scene to the North Pole characters. Shelly put them away in boxes while Mom dusted the mantel with Lemon Pledge. That was when they moved on to the serious project of stripping the tree. To make matters worse, school would be starting up tomorrow. If that didn't bring in the end of Christmas, what would? I tried to think like Aunt Loureen and convince myself that it wasn't really over, but she's better at thinking than I am.

The only thing that cheered me up was the idea of making more wishes for a while. I hadn't made any since the night Caligula talked for the first time. Aunt Loureen said I should wait before making any more wishes "to see how this present wish worked out."

"You may discover that a talking cat is not nearly as much fun as you thought," she had warned me.

"Oh, but it is."

"You like listening to a grouchy cat?"

"Sure. Sometimes he even sounds like Dad."

"No surprises there. He grew up listening to your dad, although, let's face it, cats can be pretty fussy all on their own."

"Yeah. But when Caligula gets grumpy, I'm not scared like when Dad gets grumpy."

She smiled. "I understand. And I'm grateful that so far you don't seem to be inheriting your father's temper, even if Caligula is. Still, wait a while before making your next wish."

"But we're running out of days."

"Oh nonsense. Christmas lights will last well into January. Take some time. Learn to make your choices with care."

But now I was worried about the magic ornament. If they packed it with the other boxes of Christmas decorations, it would end up in the attic. The attic was creepy with cobwebs and spiders and stuff. Some of my friends liked to explore eerie things, but they scared me and I didn't wanna have to go into a weird place like the attic to make a wish. Oh sure, I figured I might be able to magically make the spiders disappear, but there was no guarantee since Aunt Loureen said that the ornament had a mind of its own. And even if it worked, there was still the question of the bad thing. I sure hated having to think about the bad thing every time I wanted to make a wish. In the attic, something worse than spiders could come. Of course, I would be the only one in the room. I had forgotten to ask Aunt Loureen what would happen if I were all alone making a wish. It seemed to me that if the bad thing was supposed to happen to someone else in the same room, and if someone else just didn't happen to be there, maybe nothing bad would come at all. But I couldn't ask her now, so earlier in the day while my family was still taking down the outside decorations, I pretended to need a drink of water and asked if I could go into the house. I found Caligula hiding in the laundry basket, probably to get away from me and from the ornament. I carried him into the living room by the Christmas tree and made a wish. I did it with Caligula so that he could count as the "other person." I wished that I would know as much about the ornament as Aunt Loureen did. It didn't work. I felt the same and there were no new ideas in my mind, so instead, I tried another plan and wished that Caligula would know as much about the ornament as he could possibly know. This time it worked. Caligula and I had a good long talk. He told me that he hated the ornament, but yes, as a result of my wish he now knew everything. Probably he hated the ornament even more than before and that was the new bad thing. At least it seemed that way since nothing else happened. Then, when I asked him my question about wishing alone, he said he didn't know. I made an additional wish that Caligula *would know* about "lone wishes," but he still kept saying he knew nothing about it and that the ornament had given him all the information it had chosen to give.

"Try it yourself and find out," he snapped. "Just quit bugging me!"

I decided that probably the ornament only does good things when it can also do bad things, but I was too frightened to put it to the test. So, anyway, that's why I didn't wanna see it packed away in the attic.

"Say Dad," I said. "Since that ornament is a special present from Aunt Loureen, can I keep it in my room?"

"What for? It'll only break in there. It belongs with the other ornaments."

"Well...Couldn't I just keep it for a while?"

"It isn't yours," Shelly said. "Aunt Loureen gave it to all of us."

"So? I'd still like to keep it out for a while."

"I wanna keep it too!"

Even though Shelly knew nothing about the magic, I didn't like the thought of her being around the ornament all day where she could accidentally make wishes like I did with my first wish. In fact, the more I thought about it, the more I realized I needed to keep the charm as far away from her as possible. I started wondering if I shouldn't have let them pack it away instead of opening my big mouth.

"Never mind. Let's just put it in the attic."

"No!" Shelly said. "I want it."

"You didn't want it a second ago. You're just thinking about it now because I brought it up, you little copy cat."

Caligula was in the room with us, and since he knew I was the only one who could hear him, he chewed me out instantly for that comment. "Why do you people always have to describe your human shortcomings by comparing yourself to cats? When have I *ever* tried to imitate the likes of any of you? *Copy Cat* ! I'm telling you, the man who invented that phrase should be strung up by his thumbs!"

It was Mom's turn to step in, and I had a feeling things were now gonna be much worse. Whenever Mom tried to make stuff more peaceful, the whole deal was ruined.

"Now children, your Aunt Loureen would not want you fighting over this. You can share it."

"Can I share it first?" Shelly asked. "I wanna bring it to school for Show and Tell."

I was thinking of possibilities too horrible to mention. "Mom, you can't let her take it to school. She'll bust it for sure. She's such a butterfingers."

"I will not bust it. I'll be careful."

"Careful like when you dropped the dishes? Careful like when you broke Dad's aftershave lotion?"

I was hoping my comment about the aftershave would bring Dad over to my side, but he didn't seem to care much about the ornament.

"Can I, Mom?" Shelly squealed. "Can I share it first?"

"Sharing it first means you let me use it first," I said. "That's what sharing means."

"Does not. It means we take turns. And I get the first turn."

"Mom...This is a bad idea."

"I think she can take good care of it. Can't you Shelly?"

"Mom, I'm telling you..."

"Enough about the ornament!" Dad hollered.

"Thank you," said Caligula. "At long last, something the old man and I agree on."

I had to think fast. One day with that magic ornament and Shelly might just make the world come to an end. Even if she didn't, she could at least do something close to that.

"OK. Well, then I get to keep it in my room tonight since Shelly's taking it tomorrow."

"That's fair," Mom smiled. Suddenly, she tapped Dad on the shoulder. "Oh honey, look! Look at Caligula, watching us so intently. Isn't he cute?"

"Adorable," Dad muttered. "Let's finish this tree."

But Mom was still thinking about the cat. She started calling him like she always did in the same voice she used when she talked to babies. I had seen her do it a hundred times, but this would be the first time I could listen in and hear how Caligula really felt about it.

"Come here, Caligula. Come see Momma."

"Please," he said. "Not again."

"Come on, baby. Momma wants to hold her little lamb."

"Lady, you are something else."

"Oh...Stubborn today, are we?"

"No. Don't pick me up. Don't pick me...Oh man...I just had that spot all broken in."

"That's better. Now sit on my lap."

Mom sat in a chair holding the cat face to face.

"Yes. Caligula is such a good boy."

"Oh, for crying out loud!"

"Momma loves the pretty kitty. Yes she does. Yes she does. Hey! Did you see that? He took a swipe at me! Naughty, naughty baby! Naughty, naughty baby!"

"Dear God. Please make her go away."

"Park it, mister. You're not going anywhere till I hear you purr."

"You don't get it. None of you get it. We purr when we decide. We! Us! *We* decide."

❄ ❄ ❄

Later that night I sat in my room holding the ornament in my hand. It was safe for another few hours, but what then? I wanted to make a special wish, something along the lines of, "I wish that all of my sister's wishes will be ignored." But I couldn't wish alone. What could I do? Maybe I could try fetching Caligula. Boy, was he gonna be mad, but someone had to be in the room with me or nothing would work.

Everyone else was asleep. I tiptoed into the living room as quietly as I could. There he was, asleep on the sofa like always.

I grabbed him.

"Hey! What the...? You again? What now?"

"I need you."

"You're never gonna leave me alone, are you?"

He grumbled and whined all the way down the hall. I shut the door and sat him next to me on the bed.

"I'm sorry, Caligula. I mean...I know you like to sleep and all, but this is important. I think it might be dangerous if Shelly gets her hands on that ornament."

"No kidding, Sherlock. How long did it take you to figure that out?"

I laughed. "You really are funny the way you talk."

"Am I now? Well how about that?" Caligula leaped from the bed and landed right on top of my dresser. Then he turned around to face me. "I'm so glad my seething pain brings a little joy to your humdrum life."

"Look, I had no choice. You're the expert. You're an expert on the ornament."

"Only because you wished it, you miserable weasel!"

"However it happened...Now you know stuff so I need to ask you stuff. So here's my question. Can I make a one time wish that Shelly won't be able to wish things...even accidentally?"

"No," he sighed. "As your aunt told you, the ornament has a mind of its own. It doesn't like those vast, sweeping wishes. The closest you can come is to put a seal of protection over her rambunctious little thoughts."

"What good will that do?"

"It will prevent dangerous thoughts from coming into her mind. She may still accidentally wish for things, but the effect will be negligible."

"What's *negligible*?"

"I thought you were in the sixth grade, Einstein. Don't you know what the word *negligible* means?"

"Just tell me."

"It means there won't be much harm. That's the best it can do. May I go now?"

"Not yet. The main reason I brought you here is so that I could make the wish."

"Yes, of course. Another wish and another bad thing happening to me. Oh I just love this! Have you no consideration?"

"Oh come on. The only bad things that happened so far are you talking and getting angrier."

"That was when I was the focus of the wish, kid. But this is different. Now you are wishing about your sister."

"So maybe the bad thing will happen to her. Maybe the limit to her wishes will be the bad thing. You know, bad for her because she won't get what she wants."

"Your classmates never worry about you raising the curve, do they? Now let's try to pay attention. She isn't in the room! Right? So nothing bad will happen to her! I, on the other hand, *am* in the room!"

"Oh yeah! I wasn't thinking for a second."

"So there's no telling what new crisis might occur."

"I know, Caligula, but..."

"But what? What? Are you mad? If only the ornament would lose its power. If only those neighborhood Christmas lights would stop blinking because the lights in your brain certainly have."

"Well...it's just that..."

"Oh I see. It's just that I'm a cat. Yeah! Who cares what happens to ol' Caligula?"

29

I got off the bed and moved toward the dresser where Caligula was still sitting. "I do care. Honest. But all this worrying about the bad stuff that might happen…It's hard. Right now I can only think of the bad stuff that will happen when my sister gets a hold of that thing."

Caligula arched his back. "It isn't my problem. Go make the wish in front of your parents."

"I couldn't do that. I don't want something bad to happen to my parents."

"But you don't mind it happening to me. Man, I've heard everything."

"Oh come on. It may be fun. You could use a little adventure."

"And just exactly what does that mean?

"I mean you don't do much anyway. Maybe you need these wishes."

"Sure. I need these wishes like I need that idiot German Shepherd next door barking his fool head off." Caligula suddenly got a sneaky look on his face. "Hey. There's an idea. Take the ornament into the yard. Make the wish in the presence of that mangy, loud mouthed canine and let's see what happens to him."

"Naw. I'd have to get in his yard for it to work. He'll bark."

"Of course he'll bark. So wish that he can't bark. In fact…" Caligula had a gleam in his eyes. "Why not wish that he can never bark, ever again?"

"He'll bark before I have a chance and people will wake up. Too risky."

"Well I don't like risks either."

"Why not? They might spice up your life. Dad says you never move all day long."

"I? What? I never move? And just how would he know? Is he home all day? He just likes an excuse to throw me off that couch and take it himself. I never move. That's a good one."

"OK…Well…Well what did you do today before I fished you out of the laundry basket?"

"My days are full, buddy. You can be darn sure about that!"

"Give me a for instance."

"You're testing me?"

"I wanna know what you did today."

"You really think I do nothing but eat and sleep all day long, don't you?"

"Well you tell me then. What else?"

"OK…OK. This morning, another cat came into our yard."

"Yeah. I saw from the window. You didn't chase him away or anything. The two of you stared at each other for an hour."

"Listen pal, there's more to those stares than meets the eye. Important, significant communication was going on."

"Forget it. I'm sorry I said anything. But I still need to make this wish."

And then something very spooky happened. Caligula's voice sounded different, almost evil. "Kid, there's a little fact you need to get wise to. I can make wishes too. How would you like me to make a wish for myself while you're in the room? Or how would you like me to simply make a wish about you when you're not in the room?"

Caligula had never scared me like this before. I decided I'd better make the wish fast, before it was too late. "I wish that Shelly's wishes would be controlled, even when she wishes without knowing it."

"That's it!" Caligula hissed, "Now you've done it."

I picked him up and threw him out of the room fast. If he wasn't in the room, he couldn't wish. And cats can't open doors.

He shouted at me from outside. It was real loud but I'm sure my folks just heard meowing if they were hearing anything at all. "I'll get you for this, kid! I swear it!"

"Oh come on. Nothing even happened."

"Not yet. But something is *going* to happen."

"Well maybe it won't be so bad."

"It will be dreadful. I can sense it."

"How?"

"I'm a cat! That's how! Don't you know anything? Have you ever picked up a book in your life? Cats have a lot of sensory equipment. Believe me, something terrible is going to hit me and when it does, I'll pay you back. Just wait and see. I'll nail you good."

"Go to bed, Caligula."

"I *was* in bed moron! You dragged me out. But you'll regret it. You'll curse the day you messed with ol' Caligula."

"Good night."

I turned off my lights and I didn't hear any more from the other side of the door. I was very worried. If only Aunt Loureen were here. She'd know what to do. I couldn't call her because she was traveling all over England. I could write her a letter, but it would go to her home address and she wouldn't see it till she

31

got back from her trip. And she didn't have email. She didn't like computers or hardly any modern stuff.

Meanwhile, what was gonna happen to Caligula? And if it happened, what could he do to me? Maybe I could take back my wish about him talking. No, that wouldn't work. Aunt Loureen said he already knew how to talk. All I did was force it out of him. But maybe I could wish it anyway, just wish that he couldn't talk any more. That might do the trick. That would keep him from making wishes but only if the ornament allowed. It was always up to the ornament. So, if it's always up to the ornament, why did we need to wish for protection around Shelly? The ornament was already wise enough to not let her destroy the world. Was that a wasted wish? No, both Caligula and Aunt Loureen warned me about dangerous wishes.

Too many confusing thoughts were swimming in my head. I wanted to go to sleep. I wanted to wish myself to sleep, but there was no way I would bring that cat back in the room for another wish. He'd beat me to it. He'd maybe ask the ornament to turn me into a bowl of tuna and then he'd eat me. That would be the good thing for him and the bad thing for me at the same time. But only if the ornament allowed. It's all up to the ornament.

"Dear God, in heaven, please let me sleep. And please protect me from Caligula."

"Calm down," I whispered to myself just the way Aunt Loureen might have said it. "I won't ever let him near the ornament again. Without the ornament, he has no power and I'm safe. After all, he's just a cat. What could a cat really do anyway?"

Chapter Five

The Big History Question

Her name was Renee. I never knew a girl with that name before, and she was the most beautiful girl I had ever seen. Maybe it surprises you to see a sixth grader talk about stuff like love. My whole life, I'd always heard that boys don't get interested in girls till they grow older, like in high school or junior high. That was never true for me. Actually, I don't think it's true for any other boy either. I think what really happens is that younger boys are just shyer than girls, and so they pretend not to like girls. Anyway, I at least, had always liked them without admitting it.

Not that I liked every girl. Usually the ones who liked me were the ones I thought were ugly, like Patsy Peraeno, who used to chase me in first grade, trying to kiss me. Once she even cornered me when I ran into the boys' bathroom where I thought she wouldn't dare follow. I hated girls like Patsy. But there were other girls who looked real cute, like Vicky in the second grade, Phyllis and Margie in the third grade and Penny in the fourth grade. But none of the girls I knew when I was little were anything like Renee.

She transferred in as a new student before Christmas break. I noticed her good looks right off, but I never thought much about her till one morning when she overheard me telling a joke to my two best buddies at recess. She didn't laugh. She just smiled and walked by. I had never been affected by a smile before, but for some reason, when Renee smiled, I felt very strange. The smile made me take extra notice of her reddish brown hair and her pretty face and the nice looking dresses she always had on. Maybe we first like people because we think they might like us. Even if we end up being wrong, even if we realize we were imagining things, by then it's too late because now this person seems special. But I don't think I was imagining Renee liking me. Exactly why she liked me, I had no idea. Lots of people tell jokes, but I really don't tell them too well. As for looks, I figured I was sort of good looking. All my life I had been told how handsome I was, and not just from my parents. I guess brown eyes and dark wavy hair come across as handsome to folks. But still, there were many boys with wavy hair, so I wasn't sure what Renee found in me when there were so many other boys to like.

I had kind of forgotten about Renee over Christmas vacation, but that first day back at school, something happened that would keep me from ever forgetting her again.

Before I tell you the story, I should say I was usually a good student. My grades weren't great but they weren't terrible either. I always finished my homework, and I hardly ever goofed off in class or disobeyed the rules. But once in a while, when I had some reason for wanting to show off, I would make funny comments and get my classmates to laugh. I already told you that I didn't do a very good job of repeating jokes I heard. But it was different in class. My funny comments weren't actual jokes. They made people laugh because the teacher would ask a serious question, and I would give the kind of answer that wasn't expected.

Mrs. Evans was a nice, older lady who hardly ever yelled at the class. It wasn't much of a risk to say something funny to her, and I really wanted to show off for Renee, so when Mrs. Evans had us take out our history books, I started thinking of a possible clever comment. I very much wanted to see Renee smile at me again.

In the fall we had studied American History from Columbus all the way up to the Revolutionary War. Today we were continuing from where we left off.

"Class, we're going to discuss George Washington. Now you all know that he was the first President of the United States. You've heard that since kindergarten. But it may surprise some of you to learn that originally, Washington was not interested in being president. Who can tell me why he changed his mind?"

I shot my hand up.

"Yes, Mike."

"He found out that if he took the job they would put his picture on the dollar bill."

The class roared with laughter and Renee was laughing too. It had worked. I felt wonderful.

"All right, class," Mrs. Evans said to regain everyone's attention. She gave me a dry smile. "Very humorous, Mike."

Cool. I had gotten away with it. No trouble from the teacher and a cute laugh from Renee. This was going great.

"And now, Mike, you will be kind enough to tell us the real reason."

Oh brother! I really didn't know. It's not like we had read some chapter in the textbook the night before. Mrs. Evans hadn't assigned anything over the holidays. She just wanted to see what we might have already known on our own. And I knew nothing. That wouldn't have mattered if I had sat there quietly like the others, but now Mrs. Evans was about to pay me back for being such a big shot and it was gonna make me look like a real goon. I couldn't just pull the answer out of thin air...unless...Oh wow! If only I had the ornament with me now. Just imagine. "That Shelly," I said to myself. "I could kill her."

"Mike? Do you know?"

"I know, Mrs. Evans!" Barbara Driscoll said, raising her hand.

"That's fine, Barbara. But we're going to see if our class comedian can give us the answer."

This is gonna be hard to believe. It's gonna sound like one of those too good to be true stories, but I'm not kidding. At that very moment I looked out the window and actually saw my sister. The first graders had their recess at a different time than the bigger kids. There she was, the little chimp, watching her friends jump rope. She was holding the ornament too.

"Mike?"

"Ahh...I do know the answer, but can I be excused for a minute first?"

"He probably wants to run to the library to look it up," Joe Blankenship said.

The class laughed again, but this time they were laughing at Joe's comment about me instead of laughing at my clever answer. I had to fix things fast.

"Michael Owen! Do you have the answer or not?"

Now I knew she was mad. She wasn't yelling, but she called me *Michael Owen*. Teachers only use both names when they're upset. It looked like I wasn't gonna get away with this slim chance to save myself.

"I *do* know, Mrs. Evans. Honest I do. But my sister Shelly is out there having recess and I just remembered my mom wanted me to tell her that I'm walking her home today."

"Maybe he thinks his kid sister has the answer." Joe Blankenship was not gonna miss a second chance to be funny. Once again, the class busted up.

Mrs. Evans looked very suspicious. "You just now realized this? You just thought about your sister this very second while we are in the middle of a history question?"

"Well...The first grade is having recess. I saw her out the window. That's what made me think of it. Can't you hear them play? You can look out the window and see them for yourself if you want, Mrs. Evans."

"Thank you, Michael, but I'm quite familiar with the first grade recess schedule. That is hardly the point!"

This wasn't going well at all. But I didn't know how to get out of it. "It's really important, Mrs. Evans. You see, my mom has a dentist appointment. And she forgot to tell Shelly, so she told me and...and...if Shelly goes out to where my mom usually picks her up and Mom doesn't drive by, Shelly will start bawling. She's a real sensitive little girl."

I wished I were as good at history as I was at lying.

"This sounds very fishy, Michael."

"Please, Mrs. Evans."

She couldn't seem to decide what to do. "All right. But be very fast. I expect you back in less than a minute."

"Have him give the answer before he goes out."

"That will be enough, Joe. Go on, Michael. Quickly."

I ran out the door wondering what would happen if the ornament said 'no.' But why should it? Why would some ornament not want me to know history? History is good for a kid.

"Shelly...Shelly, come here."

"If you take it away from me, I'll tell Mom!"

"No. I'm not gonna take it away from you. I promise. Just come here."

She moved toward me slowly, clutching the ornament against her stomach.

"What do you want?"

"Umm...I just want to remind you to be careful."

"I *am* careful. I'm being very careful. My teacher really liked it a lot. She said it was pretty. It was the best thing at Show and Tell."

"Great. That's great." I had to make a wish without giving anything away to Shelly. I had to do it in such a way that she wouldn't suspect what was going on.

I figured it shouldn't be too hard. She was only six.

"OK...Glad you're being careful. Glad you had a good Show and Tell. I just wish things were going as well today in my class. I wish I knew my George Washington history better. See ya."

I turned toward the class room without looking back. I didn't wanna see what bad thing might happen. As I grabbed the door, I heard somebody crying. I turned around. Some little first grader had fallen down on the blacktop. Oh well. At least it wasn't Shelly and at least the kid didn't look too hurt.

❄ ❄ ❄

"He's back, Mrs. Evans!"

"Yes, Barbara. I see. Well, Michael?"

All eyes were on me, including Renee's. But I knew the answer. I actually knew. I felt like I had always known, kind of like the way Aunt Loureen felt she had always known about the ornament.

"Michael? We're waiting!"

"This oughta be good," Joe Blankenship said under his breath.

The words poured out fast and sounded just like an adult talking. But even though I was using big words, the speech felt familiar. It was very weird. "George Washington had retained his popularity as a result of unprecedented courage and overqualified leadership of the Continental Army during the American Revolution. But distaste of kings and dictators was at the heart and center of the American campaign against our mother country, England. Therefore, not wanting to be a hypocrite, not wanting to contradict his own political ideologies, Washington respectfully declined the suggestion to seek the presidency. However, when the Constitutional Convention demonstrated the numerous checks and balances which would be mandated by our Constitution and when he was made to see that a new nation needed the unifying factor of a figurehead, Washington reconsidered his position."

Every student was silent. Mrs. Evans just stood there, looking at me with her mouth half open. Renee formed a smile on her face that seemed to say, "I am so proud of you, and you're cute too." I felt a rush of joy all over.

"Mike," my teacher said, "that was fantastic!"

It sure felt good to hear her call me *Mike* again. Mrs. Evans began to clap, and everyone joined in except Joe Blankenship.

"Well Mike...I just...Well, I've never seen anything like that in my life. It's obvious you've done a lot of personal studying."

"Yeah," I lied.

"Why don't I see that vocabulary in your essays?"

I shrugged.

"Why you sounded like a teacher, you did. And not just any teacher. You sounded like a college professor. Didn't he, class?"

"Yes, Mrs. Evans," they all said together even though they had probably never heard a college professor and probably had no idea what one should sound like.

This was the best day of my life. I never knew before what I wanted to be when I grew up. Maybe I'd be a teacher like Mrs. Evans and Aunt Loureen. Maybe teaching would be my job and maybe Renee would be my wife. That ornament! That wonderful ornament! It was changing everything.

Chapter Six

Walking Home

I always walked home with my two best pals, Cliffe and Ben. Ben was in the same grade but a different class. We became friends because he lived on my street. Cliffe was in Mrs. Evans' class along with me. He was smaller than most of the other fifth graders and kind of odd looking in the face. He was also a redhead and for some reason kids always made fun of redheads. I wasn't the kind of person who called people names but I *did* want to be liked by others, so I would never have become Cliffe's friend if it hadn't been for Ben. Ben was the opposite of Cliffe in almost every way, taller, darker and stronger. Whenever we played softball during recess, Ben would choose Cliffe for his team because he felt sorry for him and he knew nobody else would choose him. Being friends with Cliffe might have made me unpopular, but after Ben took him in, it was no problem because everybody liked Ben, and that meant being cool around Ben's friends. Yeah, Ben was pretty popular. When you're good at sports, people like you. I wasn't very good at softball or basketball, but I could run fast, and I did OK at football, so people liked me better than Cliffe, but not at much as Ben.

Today, we couldn't find Ben, so Cliffe and I started walking home on our own. There was a dirt path leading from the back field of the school to a small park. A fence separated the two, and there was one spot where the fence was open, so most of the kids took this route to walk home.

"How did you do it?" Cliffe was asking me. "You really knew that answer. And you sounded different."

"Ah...It wasn't such a big deal."

"Something's going on. Come on, Mike. What are you hiding? You can tell me."

I never had time to tell him anything, because I saw Joe Blankenship up ahead with his sidekick, Brad Worley. They were pointing at us from a distance. Probably Joe was telling Brad about my history question in class. Joe was mean and he picked on kids a lot. He was also a little bigger than me, but his size wasn't the main thing that scared people. Joe was that kind of person you were afraid of, even if you didn't know why, unlike Brad Worley. Brad didn't scare people much when he was by himself. That's why he always hung around Joe. I didn't wanna be here but I wasn't sure what else to do so I kept moving and hoping for the best.

"Hey, Owen!" It was Joe calling out to me as we passed by. "Owen! Hey! I thought you were walking home with your sister!"

"Look again," Brad Worley said, pointing to Cliffe. "It *is* his sister!"

"I think they're in the mood for trouble," Cliffe whispered, sounding very frightened.

"Just ignore them."

But nobody ever got away with ignoring Joe Blankenship. He and Brad came closer and blocked our path. A few other kids started gathering around as they noticed the possible beginnings of a fight.

Joe was making up for lost time. I had been lucky up to now. He had never really taken much interest in me before. But today, he wasn't able to embarrass me in class so he was set on doing it now. "Looky here, everyone. We have an honest-to-goodness history professor. I'll bet you think you're a real tough guy now."

"Tougher than you!"

Normally I would have been too scared to say a thing like that to Joe Blankenship, but I had been feeling pretty good about myself today, and I didn't wanna ruin it all by acting like a coward. Still, I should have said something else. "Tougher than you" was a dumb thing to say to Joe Blankenship.

"Hey, Brad. What happened to the last guy who said he was tougher than me?"

"I think he's dead" Brad answered with a smile. "Oh wait! The last guy just ended up in the hospital. It's the guy before him who's dead."

Joe nodded. "So, Tough Man Owen...Where's your sister?"

"None of your business."

"That was a lie in class, right? You had to leave the room to look up the answer because you had it written down somewhere."

"How could he have done that?" Cliffe said. "Mike didn't know ahead of time what Mrs. Evans was gonna ask."

"I'm not talking to you, Frog Face!" He pushed Cliffe and knocked his books out of his hand.

"Leave him alone!" I shouted.

"Make me."

The crowd was even bigger than before. Now I was losing my nerve. I probably didn't have any real nerve to start with. I was only *acting* brave, but Joe didn't act. Joe got into real fights, and he was good. He was so good, he visited the principal's office almost every two weeks!

My only hope was to talk my way out of this without making it look like I was talking my way out of it. "We weren't bothering you. Now get out of the way!"

Joe turned to the kids who were watching. "He does *talk* tough. Let's see if he *is* tough."

Joe was now an inch from my face, grinning with glee. "You want me out of the way? You want me to stop picking on your frog friend? OK. Like I said... Make me!"

"Hey, Joe," Brad blurted out, "I think he's chicken!"

Joe shook his head. "Tsk tsk! Are you Owen? *Are* you a chicken?"

"Some pair," Brad said. "A chicken and a frog face!"

"They go together," Joe huffed. "After all, frog legs are supposed to taste like chicken."

A lot of people laughed and the crowd grew even more. I didn't see Renee yet, but she would be walking this way soon because she always walked home this way. I was real scared. If I got into a fight with Joe I would lose for sure. If I didn't fight, I'd look like a spineless jellyfish. Either way, it would ruin me in front of Renee. The best day of my life was fast turning into the worst day of my life.

Joe looked very pleased with himself. "So what are you gonna do, Owen?"

"He can't seem to talk," Brad said.

"Well now...Isn't that a shame? Maybe I should ask him about George Washington. Mr. Tough Talk knows all about George Washington. He was saying all kinds of funny stuff in class. Say something funny out here, Owen. Make us all laugh."

I froze.

"Aw," Joe continued. "Not in the mood to laugh? Maybe I'll have to do something funny myself." He reached out his hand and squeezed my nose. "If you're gonna be the class clown you need to have a red nose."

"Cut it out!" I shouted.

"Ooh," he said, pulling his hand off, "I think he's about to cry. OK, baby. Go ahead and cry. Then I'll leave you alone."

"What's going on?" It was Ben. "You looking for a fight, Blankenship?"

"This is between Owen and me. Stay out of it!"

"I'm not staying out of anything. Mike is my friend."

Ben was one of the few people who had never been picked on by Joe, probably because he was the same size and also, like I said before, Ben was good at sports. Usually if someone was good at sports, people just figured he could fight too. I wasn't sure who would really win if they actually got into a scuffle, but it didn't matter because everybody could see that Joe was afraid of him.

"Can't he fight his own battles?" Joe said to Ben.

"You're twice his size."

"I *am not* twice his size."

"Whatever. If you wanna fight someone, you can fight me."

"Hey that's not fair," Brad interrupted. "It's three against two."

"What are you talking about?" Ben said.

Joe answered. "He means there's three of you and only two of us."

He was counting Cliffe as one of us three, and everyone knew Cliffe was worthless in a fight. They weren't really scared of me either, so all they were really saying was that they didn't wanna fight Ben and Ben knew it. Heck, everybody knew it.

"No, Blankenship," Ben said. "It isn't three against two. It's one against one. You and me."

"Nope," Joe said, still keeping his cool. "I'm only gonna fight Owen. But since he's hiding behind you today, I'll take care of him tomorrow when he's all alone."

"If you do, I'll come looking for you."

"Maybe you won't need to. Maybe the baby will learn to fight for himself."

This was amazing. Joe knew how to back out of a fight without looking scared, or at least without looking *real* scared. How did he pull it off? I hadn't done nearly as good of a job of hiding my fear.

The crowd started breaking up as Joe and Brad took off. Ben slapped me on the shoulder. "You OK?"

"Yeah...Sure."

"Why didn't you guys wait for me?"

"We couldn't find you," Cliffe said. "But I sure wish we *had* waited for you."

At least I didn't cry. I almost did. Joe was right about that. But I didn't. And I was glad Ben came along before Renee did. There was a lot to be grateful for, but I still felt pretty crummy. I had wanted to stand up to him. I started to and then I got so scared I could hardly move. Tomorrow everyone would be talking about it. Renee might find out too. But tomorrow would be different. Tomorrow I wasn't gonna need Ben or anyone else to protect me from Joe Blankenship because tomorrow, I was returning to school with the ornament hidden in my pocket.

Chapter Seven

Dealing With Shelly

"I'm home Mom!"

"She's out back," Shelly said. "She's working in her garden. She left some milk and cookies for you and Cliffe."

Cliffe usually stayed at my house for a while after school. Ben went home to get a head start on his homework but Cliffe always stayed. I think Cliffe liked our parents better than his own even though he did complain that my dad yelled a little too much. But he usually left before Dad got home from work anyway, so it didn't matter.

"Help yourself, Cliffe," I said, pouring myself a glass of milk. Cliffe sat down at the dining room table and picked up a sandwich cookie.

"Hey!" Shelly said. "You're not supposed to eat the middle out first!"

"He can eat them any way he wants," I said. "And how come you're still holding the ornament? Time to give it back."

"Uh uh...Today is my turn. Mom said."

"Your turn was at school. Now it's my turn."

"Is not! I get it the whole day! You don't get it till tomorrow!"

"Can I see it?" Cliffe asked.

Shelly held it up, but she wouldn't let go of it.

"An ornament." Cliffe took a sip of milk and then put his glass down. "Why are you guys fighting over an ornament?"

"Our Aunt Loureen said it has a special charm," Shelly blurted out.

"What special charm?"

"Nobody knows. But I'm gonna find out soon."

I didn't like the sound of that. Something wasn't right. "Hand it over," I said.

"No. I like it. I'm gonna ask Mom if I can keep it."

"You can't keep it."

"Why not?" Shelly got up from the table and moved toward the kitchen holding on to the ornament like she was afraid I would take it.

I followed her. "We already explained, Dopey. Aunt Loureen gave it to the whole family. Just what happened in school today anyway?"

I *was* curious. Obviously the world hadn't come to an end. But something must have happened. That ornament was so powerful and Shelly had such a big mouth, something must have happened.

"I already told you. I brought it for Show and Tell."

"Did you say anything about the magic charm?"

"Yeah. But nobody believed me."

"Of course nobody believed you. What did you go and say a dumb thing like that for?"

"Aunt Loureen says it has a charm!"

"I know. But people aren't gonna believe that."

"Your aunt always has these strange stories, doesn't she?" Cliffe said, reaching for a second cookie.

"Yeah." I turned back to Shelly. "So you said Show and Tell went well?"

"Uh huh. Billy Fletcher laughed when I told them about the charm, but then he suddenly started coughing."

"Did you tell him to stop laughing?"

"No. But my teacher did. She said, 'Billy, I wish you wouldn't make fun of people during Show and Tell,' and suddenly he had this real bad cough. He had to leave the room to get a drink of water."

"Oh brother..." I thought to myself. "It's a wonder we're all alive today."

"And then at recess Timmy pulled it out of my hand to look at it."

"What happened?"

"I called the teacher."

"What did she do?"

"She told him to give it back. He said he just wanted to look at it."

"Yeah? And then what?"

She said, "Well, I wish you'd ask first."

I was afraid to hear what happened next, but Shelly went right on talking.

"Then he asked real polite. But he already took it out of my hand. He gave it back right away, though, 'cause he suddenly noticed that his fly was unzipped."

I laughed.

"They were new pants that he had for his birthday. That's probably why he forgot to zip them. But he brought birthday cake, and we sang him happy birthday in class and my teacher lit candles and..."

"Oh no..." I said to myself.

"And then he made a birthday wish."

"What did he wish for?"

"I don't know, silly. He made it to himself. If you say it out loud it doesn't come true."

"Sometimes it does."

"Does not."

"Well, did he whisper it?"

"Sure he whispered it. But nobody could hear."

"Well...any other good things happen today?"

"Umm...Let's see...Our teacher didn't give us any homework. That was good."

Now I knew what little Timmy had wished for. "No homework, huh?"

"No. Mrs. Waterman cut her finger with the cake knife by accident. So I think she forgot about the homework 'cause she was busy putting on a bandage."

She'd had some interesting adventures all right, but it looked like she still hadn't figured out the charm. In fact, it sounded like she hadn't made any wishes at all. Everyone around her shot their mouths off, but not Shelly. Then why was she so sure about learning the charm? I needed to keep her talking.

"Well...Exciting day..."

"It sure was. I had so much fun. I wish I could..."

Oh no! This was as horrible a thing as could possibly happen. Shelly was about to use the magic by accident. She was about to wish that she could take the ornament to school every day. I snatched it out of her hand.

"Mom!"

Good. Let her scream. Let her be a tattle-tale. And while she did that, she would be distracted and too upset to think about wishing.

Shelly ran into the back yard to fetch Mom.

Cliffe looked up from the table. "What's with you today? Everything you've done all day is weird."

"We need to get to my room fast."

"Huh?"

"I'll explain later. Just hurry up. This way."

I could hear Shelly bawling in the back yard. "And he grabbed it out of my hand...And I didn't do nothing to him."

"Didn't do *anything*," Mom corrected.

"Mom's gonna be calling me out there any second," I said to Cliffe. "Come on...This way."

I opened my bedroom door and rushed inside.

"What are you doing, Mike?"

"I just wanna make sure the cat isn't in here."

"The cat? What does your cat have to do with anything?"

"Just a sec..." I opened the closet door. "Ok. Coast is clear. Hey Cliffe! Shut the bedroom door!"

"Michael! Come out here to the back yard please!" Her voice was coming through my bedroom window because my window was by the back yard.

I put the ornament in my top dresser drawer.

"What's the deal with that ornament?" Cliffe asked.

"Never mind. I have to talk to Mom. Let's go back out."

"I'll wait here."

"No. Come with me."

48

"Mike, what's this all about?"

"I said I'll explain later."

"Well I'm staying in here. I don't wanna listen to your mom yell at you."

"OK. Stay here if you want. But if the cat walks by, you're not to let him in. Understand?"

"What difference does the cat make?"

"Just don't let him in!"

"OK."

"Mike!"

"You better go. Your mom's getting sore."

❅ ❅ ❅

Mom was sitting on a lawn chair, holding Shelly on her lap. "Michael, did you grab that out of her hand?"

"No."

"Did so! He's lying."

"No, Mom, I did take it, but I didn't mean to grab it. She *has* had it all day and she was being selfish."

"I have half a mind to put that ornament up in the attic like your father suggested."

"No, Mom. I get to keep in my room for a while. You promised."

Shelly sniffed and wiped her nose. "Well you aren't in your room during school, so I'll take it to school every day."

"You will not!"

"I will if Mom says I can. Can I Mom?"

"Mom, you should hear all the stories she told about people grabbing it out of her hand. Do you know how many times that thing could have been broken?"

"Right now I'm concerning myself with just one person who may have grabbed it out of her hand, Michael."

"I didn't, Mom…Honest…She just thinks that because she's become a real hog with that ornament."

"Only Timmy grabbed it at school."

"Shelly, you can't take it to school every day. Mike is right about that. It'll just get broken."

Shelly started crying.

"You always think you can get your way by bawling. Don't fall for it, Mom."

"That's enough...OK, Mike, keep the ornament in your room for one day. Then it goes back to the attic."

I had bought some time. And a little time was all I needed. Tomorrow I would make up some story about why I took the ornament to school. Sixth graders were too old for Show and Tell, so I would make up some other reason for bringing it with me and offer that instead of my real reason, Joe Blankenship. Then, as part of the story, I would pretend to have lost the ornament. Meanwhile, it would stay hidden in my room. I might get in trouble for losing it, but that was OK. I'd just make a wish. I'd wish that I didn't get in trouble.

Chapter Eight

Caligula and the Bad Thing

When I made my wish about Caligula talking, I thought all the ornament would do was force him to speak English, "a talent cats already had," according to Aunt Loureen. But there was something about the way I worded my wish that allowed me to hear Caligula constantly. Even when he only made cat calls, the sounds somehow turned themselves into words for my ears.

I heard it mostly when he was hungry. Usually Mom fed the cat every morning. Dad woke up before Mom to get ready for work. He always ignored the cat and Caligula had given up long ago on getting anything from Dad. But Mom was an easy touch. Caligula would meow and meow at her door till she got out of bed and placed two bowls on the kitchen floor, one filled with canned food and one with crunchies.

This morning, his voice was so loud, it woke me up even though he was standing by Mom's bedroom. Mom heard meowing. I heard, "Feed me! Feed me! Feeeeeeeeeeeeeed me!!!!! Come on lady! Rise and shine! Let's go! Up and at 'em!"

I headed for Mom's room and picked Caligula up. He was *not* happy to see me.

"Hey, this doesn't concern you. It's between me and your old lady."

She opened her door, looking very tired.

"I'll feed him today, Mom."

"Thank you, honey. That's very sweet of you."

I headed for the kitchen with Caligula in my arms.

"Good morning, Caligula."

"If you say so."

"Well, what can I get you today? Tuna? Chicken? Liver?"

"What are you doing? What's going on?"

"I just..."

"Are we pretending to be a waiter? Is that it? Gonna tell me about the soup of the day next?"

"What's your problem?"

"Have you ever asked me before? I don't do the menu thing. Just put something in the bowl and shove it on the floor for Pete's sake!"

"You sure are a grouch."

"Oh spare me! I mean, who are we kidding? You ask me these stupid questions just to hear me talk. You don't really care what I have for breakfast!"

"Have it your way," I said, grabbing a can out of the cupboard. "I thought we could make peace."

Caligula's tail was twitching. "Oh that's it. You're trying to butter me up. It's a little late for that. I said I'd pay you back and I will."

"Pay me back for what? Nothing has happened."

"It will!"

I found the can opener and opened up Caligula's breakfast. I hadn't looked at the label since he said he didn't care what I gave him, but now I could smell the stuff. It was tuna and it really reeked. I never could see how cats stomached food like this. It made me glad to be a human being. I scraped it into his red bowl on the floor. He darted toward his food and started chomping loudly. It was strange to see this kind of normal, regular, old animal behavior after all that had happened the last few days. Caligula may not have been a talking cat, but he was still a cat. I opened the bag of dried food and poured some of it into his other bowl, the blue one.

"All right. Just go ahead and eat. After you're finished, I have some more ornament questions for you."

He looked up for a second, licking his chops. "Oh goody! Something to look forward to after breakfast. I was really hoping we could talk about the ornament some more."

While he ate, I showered and got dressed for school. Then I gathered my books together. I was not gonna take out the ornament until Caligula and I were done talking. There were about fifteen minutes to spare. Mom had left to drop Shelly off. I always waited for my friends and walked to school.

Caligula was finished now. As he cleaned himself, I went through my first day back at school and told the cat everything.

"Now here's my question."

"Yes," he said, yawning deliberately.

"Sometimes the bad thing makes sense, kind of like it's part of the wish. Other times, stuff just happens, like the first grader falling down."

"If I explain, will you beat it and leave me alone?"

"Yeah...sure."

"All right then. If what you're wishing about gives you pleasure at someone else's expense, than that obviously is the good thing and the bad thing at the same time."

"Hmm...I see...So when I accidentally wished that Aunt Loureen would understand..."

"It was at the expense of her becoming a post-dated liar. And when you wished for me to talk..."

"I know, I know. You didn't want to. You've told me a million times. What about the lima beans? I just wanted them to be gone. They didn't have to show up on Shelly's plate."

"No, they didn't *have to* in that case, but somebody in the room was going to be affected and you were already angry at Shelly for snitching on you, so the ornament channeled things her way."

"I see. Yeah, I get it. Well then, what about the first grader who fell down?"

"That George Washington wish was only about you. It was not at anyone else's expense."

"Maybe not. But I *was* mad at someone. I was mad at Joe Blankenship."

"I know. But he wasn't outside with you. He was still in the classroom. So the ornament hit some other kid at random. Are you catching on or do I need to draw you a picture? How many more times do we have to go through this?"

"OK, OK. I get it."

"Do you also get the part about not hurting others? I distinctly remember your Aunt telling you to make those wishes responsibly."

"I'm trying."

"You call that 'trying'? Making some poor yahoo fall over just so you can show off in class for that red headed girl?"

"He wasn't hurt!"

"Of course not. That's why he cried. He cried because he *wasn't* hurt. Good one."

"I mean he wasn't hurt bad. And I didn't make him fall. The ornament did."

"Sure, sure. Blame the ornament when people get hurt; take the credit when the ornament makes you look like a genius in class."

"What about you? You don't seem to care who gets hurt. What about when you kill birds and mice?"

"That's different. That's survival. I kill them only so I can eat."

"You don't need to eat them. You get tuna and chicken and liver. All you want."

"Oh man, there's just no talking to you."

Mom walked through the front door, returning from taking Shelly to school. "Mike? Can I speak with you?"

"Sure."

Mom sat down. From the way she looked, I knew this wasn't gonna be good news. "It's about Caligula."

The cat glared at me.

"What about him?"

"Well, I wanted to wait until Shelly was gone because what I have to say will really upset her, and we need to find a special way to tell her."

"This is it," Caligula said. "I curse that ornament. I curse it!"

Mom continued. "As you know, your father has wanted to get rid of Caligula for quite some time because of the way he scratches up the furniture."

"Yeah. But you told Dad there was no way."

"I did. Yes, I love Caligula. At first I put my foot down and your father dropped the matter. But he keeps bringing the matter back up. It has created a lot of tension in the house. I was hoping Jim would change the way he feels, but instead, he complains more each day. Your father does come first. He's my husband after all, and Caligula…"

"Don't say it," he hissed.

"And Caligula is just a cat."

The cat had hatred in his eyes. "Well I hope you're satisfied!" he said to me. "Are you going to just sit there looking like a tree stump? Say something!"

"Mom, you can't let him do it!"

"Sweetie, I never knew you cared that much about the cat."

"Well...He's kind of grown on me."

"You'll have to do better than that, kid. Scratch post. Tell her to just buy a scratch post. Easy problem. Easy solution."

"Couldn't we just get a scratch post?"

"Your father doesn't want a scratch post in the living room."

"Hey Mike!" Cliffe and Ben were calling my name from the front porch like they did every school day.

"Your friends are here. We'll talk more after you get home. It'll probably be a day or two before anything is done."

"You gonna give him away, Mom?"

"I don't think so, honey. Maybe we'll try to find him a nice home first, but when people decide to get a new pet, they usually want kittens, not full grown cats. So, in all likelihood, we'll be taking him to the pound."

Caligula buried his face in his paws. Aunt Loureen had guessed that he might just end up in the pound. She sure was a smart aunt.

"But Mom, doesn't the pound only keep them for a few days and then kill them if they aren't chosen?"

"Mike! Come on! We need to get going!" My friends were getting impatient.

Mom looked like she was about to cry. "We'll talk more later."

I picked up Caligula and walked toward the hallway.

"Where are you taking him?"

"Could you let Cliffe and Ben in? I just wanna be with Caligula for a sec."

But I took him to the den since the ornament was in my dresser drawer. I wasn't gonna let Caligula near it, not in the mood he was in, not with the threats he had made.

"You need to stay in here till I leave with the ornament."

"For a minute I thought you brought me in here to console me. But all you care about is your own safety and your own greed."

"Well you're the one who threatened to use it against me, so what else do you expect me to do?"

Caligula jumped up on the window sill and looked out the window. I think he had heard a bird or something. I was surprised that he could think about stuff like that while we were having such a serious chat. But I guess he was able to do both at the same time because he went right on talking while his head bobbed back and forth, following whatever had caught his attention outside.

"You may be able to keep me separated from the ornament for now, but sooner or later you'll slip up. You'll be careless and stupid because you are a careless, stupid kid. And when it happens, I'll be waiting."

I walked over to the window. "Hey this may not even be part of the wish. You may have caused your own problem. Why are you always scratching up the furniture anyway?"

"Because I'm a cat. Cats do those kinds of things. And it certainly *is* related to the wish. I've been listening to your dad gripe about me for years. And by some incredible coincidence your mother just now decides to do what he wants? Get real! This is your fault, all right."

I sat down at the desk by the bookshelf. "Look, I'm sorry. I'll think of something. I promise. I won't let them take you to the pound."

"The pound. Every dog and cat lives in terror of that place, that animal concentration camp, that extermination center. And now, here I am, headed right for it. And for what? I scratched some furniture. Great big crime! For years your dad complains that I never do anything. So now I did something. I scratched the furniture. This is a nightmare! That's what it is, a nightmare!"

"I said I'll take care of it."

"Whew! That's a relief. And you take care of things so well. No, kid, I don't think you'll take care of it, but I'm gonna take care of you. Mark my words!"

"Stop trying to scare me! Look, I don't have time right now. When I get home from school, we'll figure something out. Maybe I can make another wish I'll wish for Dad to change his mind and start liking you."

"You can't undo a wish that's already been made."

"Who says so?"

"I do. You made me the expert. Remember? You cannot undo a wish or the bad effect of a wish."

"Then we won't use the ornament. We'll try something else. There must be things we can do without using magic. Now I really need to leave."

He jumped off the window sill, ran toward the door and blocked my way.

"Leave! Sure! Leave! Off to school! Off to make more wishes!"

"So what if I am?"

"Hey, why don't you just get rid of that thing? It's dangerous and you don't know how to use it."

"Mike!" Mom was calling me from the living room. "You're late and you're making your friends late!"

"I'm coming!" I knelt down next to Caligula. "I'll see you later. Hey, I know! Just run away. Mom doesn't know you heard her. She has no reason to keep an eye on you."

"Just run away." He placed one of his paws on my knee and dug in. "Kid, where do stray cats end up?"

"I don't know."

"IN THE POUND!!!!!"

"Well, maybe when you get to the pound you can talk. Nobody will kill a talking cat. And lots of people would love to own a talking cat."

"You have no idea what you're saying, do you? You just ramble on and on, flapping your lips and leaving your brain at the starting gate. First of all, I'd be blacklisted by cats everywhere. Our abilities are well kept secrets, held in sacred trust."

"Yeah. But if your life's at stake…"

"And then, even if I wanted to talk, I can't now, thanks to you."

"Me?"

"Because of that fatal wish, only you can hear me now when I *do* speak. Man, you fixed everything real good, didn't you?"

"There's always hope."

"Oh? Well there'd just better be! Because even though you're a pin head, you *are* my only hope!" His voice got low and very threatening. "Get them to change their minds. Do something. Do it fast and do it skillfully. Because if I go down, I'm taking you down. And if you think I'm not able, because I'm 'only a cat,' well, you just try me."

I locked him in. With Caligula safe in the den, I rushed to my own room and pulled the ornament out of my drawer. He was right. I did seem to be making a mess of things. Not using the charm anymore was starting to sound like a good idea. But I just had to use it again for protection against Joe Blankenship. As for Caligula, I would deal with him later. One problem at a time.

Chapter Nine

Joe Blankenship Versus The Ornament

We had only walked a few feet from the house when my friends stopped dead in their tracks and stood on each side of me.

"Hey, what gives?"

"I'll tell you what gives," Ben said. "We're your friends."

"Yeah? So?"

"So you've been keeping a secret from us," Cliffe added.

"Cliffe told me everything, Mike, about that history question, about the Christmas ornament. Now what's going on?"

"Nothing."

"There's something spooky about the ornament," Cliffe insisted.

"Forget the ornament. It's just a present from my aunt. It annoys my dad, so I don't like to see Shelly waving it around."

Cliffe shook his head. "Why would your dad be annoyed by an ornament?"

"He just is. And Shelly took it to school yesterday for Show and Tell. That's all."

Cliffe wasn't buying it. "But why did you need to talk to Shelly before you answered the history question? I mean, I hate Joe Blankenship, but he was right. You were lying about walking Shelly home. And Shelly had the ornament at school. And when we got back to your house yesterday, you grabbed the ornament out of her hand and practically ran to your room to hide it in your dresser."

"Aw...I told you. I like the ornament, but it annoys my dad, so I was just keeping it out of sight."

"Look, Mike," Ben said. "We aren't going anywhere till you level with us."

"We'll be late."

"I don't care. Tell us about the ornament."

"There's nothing to tell. Forget the ornament."

"What's that in your pocket?"

"Nothing."

"Come on, Mike. Open up your pocket or we'll do it ourselves."

I couldn't risk breaking the glass, so I took it out.

Ben shook his head. "Forget the ornament, huh? OK. Start from the beginning."

"We're gonna be late!"

"Then you'd better talk fast."

It was lunch time. I was sitting on a bench with Ben and Cliffe. I couldn't even think about eating, but out of habit I opened my paper bag to see what my mom had packed: peanut butter and jelly sandwich, barbecued potato chips, and an apple.

I looked around for Joe but I didn't see him yet. There was a teacher on yard duty, but fights usually got going long before she saw what was happening. Joe would be coming for sure. All through class he kept grinning at me from across the room.

It felt good to have friends like Cliffe and Ben by my side. I had actually enjoyed telling them the story of the ornament. It's hard keeping a secret, and I was glad to have some company. Ben had a rough time believing at first, but Cliffe had been there during history which made him a pretty good second witness and also, the very fact that I had not wanted to say anything, somehow made it all the easier for Ben to believe when I finally coughed it up.

"Hi, Mike." It was Renee.

I felt like I could hardly breathe. Renee, talking to me!

"I just wanted to say, I thought you were wonderful in class yesterday."

Cliffe and Ben were both enjoying this, but Cliffe was smiling more.

"Aw, that," I said. "It was nothing."

"You must be very smart."

"Aw...I know a few things."

We stared at each other. I could see that she was just as uncomfortable as me. But that was good 'cause it meant she was hung up on me.

"Well...I'll be seeing you."

"Sure, Renee. See ya around."

She walked away slowly and looked back once in my direction.

"Man, is she stuck on you!" Cliffe said.

I just shrugged.

"Don't act like you didn't notice." He started acting it out. "Oh Mike, you were wonderful in class."

Ben shoved him. "Lay off! At least girls talk to him."

"Oh no," Cliffe said pointing across the yard. "Here they come."

I saw Joe from a distance with Brad strutting along beside him. I took the ornament out of my pocket. Aunt Loureen said I didn't need to touch it while making wishes, but I wanted to at least have one last look because I was getting so scared, I was afraid I might feel too nervous to concentrate on my wish.

"Guys, it's time for you to leave."

"Let me handle this for you, buddy."

"No Ben. Please. If you do, everyone will call me a chicken. I wanna take care of him myself."

"And you're gonna do it with *that*?" he said pointing to the ornament.

"I hope so. That's what we all agreed on. Look, just go across the yard a little. If they see you with me, they won't come over."

"They already see us."

61

"Then beat it. Both of you. I mean it. Go back toward the cafeteria for a few minutes. You can always come back when they aren't looking."

Ben sighed. "I hope you know what you're doing. Come on, Cliffe."

Ben and Cliffe walked away as Joe and Brad moved closer. I knew exactly what to wish because I'd rehearsed it the night before. I really wanted to clean Joe's clock, but I had to be careful, like Aunt Loureen always warned me. She said the ornament wouldn't kill anyone or make anyone sick, but she had also added "as a general rule," so I practiced my words over and over again in my mind to make sure the ornament didn't pull some trick to punish me for phrasing the wish poorly. I had gone over it about twenty times, and I knew the exact words by heart. If all went as planned, some very good things were about to happen to me and some very bad things were about to happen to Joe at the same time.

"I wish that I can be powerful enough to hurt Joe Blankenship...Ah...Ah... But without him dying or getting sick or getting crippled, or anything like that... And I also wish that if he insults me, I can insult him back and say something real clever right in front of the other kids...And... And I wish that I won't be afraid of him."

I still felt scared. That was already one of my three wishes that the ornament must have quickly said 'no' to. But I half expected that one. Probably nothing could change the way a person actually feels, not even a powerful charm. But the other two wishes, what would happen to me if they weren't granted? I also hoped the ornament would view my requests as two parts of the same wish so that only one bad thing would happen instead of two bad things. Maybe the ornament would view them that way. But it was hard to guess what this crazy device might decide to do.

"Hey look, Brad. He talks to himself!"

Other kids started pointing and crowding around. News of our fight had spread fast and many sixth graders were looking forward to it. Renee also noticed from across the blacktop. She and a girlfriend moved toward the crowd. I was hoping she wouldn't see this 'cause I didn't know for sure what the ornament would do.

"Good morning, baby," Joe smiled. "Are we gonna fight today or cry?"

"I never cried!"

"You almost did. You were about to."

"Hey!" Brad said. "Look at that toy he's holding!"

Joe moved in. "What ya got there, baby? A rattle?"

"It's a Christmas ornament. Don't you know the difference between a rattle and a Christmas ornament? I sure wouldn't wanna send you to the store!"

A few people laughed, but not too many. I didn't blame them. Who wanted to get on Joe Blankenship's bad side? My words were brave, even if my feelings weren't. Maybe the ornament was working, but I wasn't sure. After all, I had talked tough yesterday at first. But right now I was also saying clever things, and although I had said clever things before, I had never said them while I felt this frightened. Besides, the words just seemed to pour out and that reminded me very much of my magic George Washington answer. Yeah, the ornament had to be working.

"Very funny, professor. But it still looks like a toy. What are you doing with an ornament anyway? Didn't you hear that Christmas was over?"

"What are you doing with that face?" I replied. "Didn't you hear that Halloween was over?"

This time everyone laughed, including Renee. Joe looked embarrassed, which meant he was gonna do something fast. I put the ornament in my pocket so that both of my hands could be free.

"OK, Owen. Let's see what *your* face looks like when I'm done with you."

He charged. I lifted my hands as kind of a reflex. Suddenly something which looked like small bolts of lightning shot out of my fingertips. Joe instantly fell over as several girls screamed. Everything happened so fast, it almost didn't seem real.

"What's going on here?" It was the yard duty teacher, well timed as always. I looked up at her and then I looked down at Joe. He was lying on the blacktop completely still, and I had no idea if he was alive or not.

Renee? Oh yeah! I cared about Renee. I would care about her no matter what. I wasn't sure what made me think about all these things when I was in the middle of a conversation with Mrs. Harold. It happened to me a lot. One single event would make me think of all kinds of other stuff.

"So how did it happen? How did Joe end up lying on the ground?"

"I just hit him," I lied. "That's all. I hit him." I wasn't about to try explaining lightning coming out of my fingertips.

"Some of the kids said something about an electric shock. What were they referring to?"

I shrugged.

"Michael Owen, are you carrying some kind of weapon?"

"No ma'am."

"Because if you *are* carrying a weapon, you will be suspended. You are aware of that, aren't you? You are aware that a weapon means an automatic suspension?"

"I know."

"You know what?"

"I know a weapon means suspension. I didn't use any weapon."

"Then what was all that talk about an electric shock?"

I shrugged.

"If I were you, young man, I'd stop shrugging and start cooperating. What is that in your pocket?"

"Nothing."

"Empty your pockets please."

"I don't have a weapon in my pocket!"

"Do as I say, Mr. Owen!"

Mr. Owen sounded even worse than *Michael Owen*.

It might have been funny to pull out my harmless looking Christmas ornament when she was expecting to see some kind of stun gun. But I had a feeling that if Mrs. Harold saw the ornament she would keep it. Even though that made no sense, this lady would keep it and have it examined by an expert or something. I was positive. I bent my head over and started whispering a wish.

"Did you hear me? What are you doing?"

"I'm praying."

"This isn't a church! I'm talking to you!"

Mrs. Harold was one of those principals who didn't like prayer at school. For some reason she thought that if some kids were praying, that meant the other kids would lose all of their rights. I didn't understand, but I didn't understand half of the rules grown ups made. Anyway, I really did feel like praying. Somehow right now, God seemed like a friendlier person to take my troubles to than this sneaky ornament. But even though I felt that way, I *wasn't* praying. It was a fake prayer so that she wouldn't hear me whisper.

And this is what I whispered. "I wish that the ornament would disappear from here and magically re-appear at home in my bedroom drawer. I wish that when I empty my pockets, the ornament would be gone."

It worked. The ornament did disappear.

"I said, empty your pockets now!"

I stood up and let the inside of my pockets out. Except for some loose change, and a few puree marbles, there was nothing in there.

"OK. Sit down."

I wondered what the bad thing would be. Something bad was gonna happen soon.

"We called your father. He's on his way."

That was bad all right. Wait. That sounded like a bad thing for me, and the bad thing couldn't happen to me. It could only happen to Mrs. Harold because she was the only one in the room with me when I made the wish. Maybe my dad would take my side and chew her out. He might. Actually, Dad didn't mind me being in fights. He used to always teach me to stand up for myself even though I didn't ever do it till today. Yeah, my dad's visit was gonna be worse for Mrs Harold than for me.

"It's a grave situation, Mr. Owen, a very grave situation."

This time, *Mr. Owen* was my dad, not me. But I was in the room with them. Mrs. Harold had been talking since he got here, without Dad hardly saying a word. Now, finally, he was ready to speak.

"You say the kid's all right?"

"Yes. Fortunately, Joe only remained unconscious for a second. The nurse has checked him out and sent him home for the rest of the day."

"OK, well then, if the kid is all right, what's the problem? What's the commotion?"

Mrs. Harold looked surprised. I think she expected more support from my dad. "For one thing, poor Joe has had quite a scare."

"So has my son, Mrs. Harold. He looked terrified when I first walked into your office."

"As well he should. I scolded him good! We don't approve of fighting at this school, Mr. Owen."

"My son said the other boy started it, and my son doesn't lie."

I started thinking about all the lies I had told since the ornament came into my life.

"Mr. Owen, I know that Joe starts a lot of fights. I don't care who started it."

"Oh? Well I do."

Usually I hated the way Dad was always in a bad mood and always putting people down. But right now I loved it. I was rooting for him all the way because this time, I hadn't lied. Joe *did* start the fight.

"Mr. Owen, fighting is serious."

"Now listen to me carefully, ma'am. No weapon was found on my son. That's what you told me. He was dragged here by one of your own teachers right from the scene of the fight which means there was no time to hide this imaginary stun gun you keep bringing up. The other boy is all right. Everything is fine. That means everything is over with. That means the matter has been settled, and I expect the school to act as though the matter has been settled. And if by chance some kind of bad publicity gets out about my son, if I should happen to read about this in the papers or see it on the six o'clock news, or hear some talking head psychologist analyze the situation on cable, I will file a lawsuit against your school that will make people wish they had a principal who had handled the matter more discretely."

Mrs. Harold looked like somebody had hit *her* with a stun gun.

Dad continued. "I've said my piece. You were honest with me. I hope you fully understand how honest I am being with you. I just hope you do."

At first she said nothing. I had never seen a school principal so quiet.

Finally she spoke in a much lower voice. "You're probably right. There probably was no weapon. I interrogated your son to double check, to be extra cautious. I'm sure you understand." She offered Dad a weak smile. Dad didn't smile back. She continued. "We must still talk to a few students who thought they saw something, but I promise the matter will be handled discretely."

"See that it is!"

"However, Mr. Owen, fighting is still serious in its own right. And that was always my bigger concern here. Weapon or no weapon, your son knocked somebody unconscious. That shows quite a temper, quite a fit of rage. I would think such a thing would alarm you."

I couldn't believe she had the nerve to take my dad on for another round. I guess principals aren't used to losing arguments, not even scared principals. But she was gonna lose this one.

"I taught the boy to defend himself. He just did what I taught him and I'm proud of him."

I don't think Dad ever said he was proud of me before. If he had, I couldn't remember.

"You're proud? Proud that a child in grade school is fighting?"

"He won't be in grade school for long. As he gets older, the bullies get bigger and more dangerous."

"Mr. Owen, surely you're concerned about all the violence in schools these last few years."

"Everyone's concerned, madam. So maybe the school should do something about it. Just where was the teacher on yard duty? How is it that she didn't see anything until the fight was all over?"

"Now, Mr. Owen, that isn't fair. Our school yard is very crowded. She did the best she could. Our teachers are overworked and underpaid."

"So am I, Mrs. Harold. So am I. But no matter how underpaid I am, it seems my tax dollars are still paying for your teachers. And if my own money can't pay for some yard duty twit to stop fixing her hair long enough to stay alert and do her job and protect my son, well, then, I won't lose any sleep if he protects himself. Now, I'm a busy man. And if this was a hard day for the bully, it was even harder on Michael, because he was picked on by poor helpless Joe, then tried and judged without a jury. So now, I'd like to take *him* home unless you'd care to also blame him for the school's low test score averages or the shortage on school milk!"

Mrs. Harold was almost in tears. Yeah, this was the bad thing all right. Funny how that ornament worked. These were Dad's real words. I knew Dad well and I knew how he really talked. It wasn't magic, like when the ornament gave me my George Washington answer or my clever words for Joe. I guess the ornament didn't always do magic. Sometimes the ornament just used people's real personalities. The ornament was clever. It knew that no magic on earth could make Mrs. Harold feel worse than my dad was making her feel.

But right now, I wasn't rooting for Dad any more. Now I was feeling sorry for Mrs. Harold. Dad was always griping about how bad the public schools were, but mostly I liked it here. I liked the teachers too. Besides, everybody knew that no adult can ever keep kids from getting into a fight. Yard duty teachers always showed up after the fights got going. How do they know when a fight is gonna start?

The drive home seemed long even though we lived real close to the school. Dad pulled the car up in the driveway and turned off the engine. I started to open the door.

"Just a minute," Dad said. "I want to talk to you."

I was frightened. When Dad said he wanted to talk to me, it usually meant that he wanted to yell at me.

But he didn't yell. "Son, I'm sorry you had such a troublesome day. It must have been very hard on you."

I broke down and started sobbing. Dad took me in his arms and held me tight. "It's OK. It's OK. Go ahead and cry. Get it all out."

Strange. For the last two days, I'd done everything I could to keep myself from crying at school and looking like a baby in front of the other kids. But this was a different kind of crying. This was a kind of crying that felt good. I didn't understand. I just knew. It was different.

After I settled down, Dad spoke to me. "You did well today. I *am* proud of you, like I said. But maybe it would be better next time to punch the other boy in the stomach. That still hurts but it isn't quite so dangerous and it doesn't usually knock him on the ground like a punch in the jaw does. I assume you hit him in the jaw or the face. That's what made him fall over. Right?"

"Yeah. I hit him in the face." Too late to change the story now. Besides, Dad would get mad again if I started telling him about the ornament. And I liked him this way, not mad. I didn't wanna hear him go on and on about "Aunt Loureen and her tall tales."

"Well, Son, up until today, you hadn't shown much of a temper. I want you to defend yourself, yes, but I *was* hoping you wouldn't pick up my bad temper. It's OK. I'm not blaming you. It's my fault. I haven't been the best influence. I know I yell a lot, far too often. I know I scare you even though I don't mean to. I don't know why I fly off the handle so much. My life hasn't been an easy one. But that's no excuse, no excuse to make *your* life miserable. I want things to be easier for you. I want you to have better opportunities. I want you to be happy. I want your life to be more enjoyable than mine, easier than mine. All fathers want that for their sons, at least, all good fathers. When I see you making the same kinds of mistakes I used to make, well, it's just as though it's me doing it all over again. You're a part of me, Son. I know it's been a while since you've heard me say this, but I do love you. I love you more than you can possibly imagine."

I had no idea what made Dad go on and on like that. I'd never heard him talk this way before. But I was about to hear the biggest surprise of all.

"I never knew my father, or my mother. I never told you this. I was adopted. Your grandmother and grandfather; they aren't my real parents. I mean, of course they're my real parents because they raised me and loved me. They're the only parents I've ever known."

The news didn't bother me. It was just unexpected. That's all.

"What about Aunt Loureen? Is she your real sister?"

"Well, again, she's the only sister I ever knew, my big sister who took great care of me. Grandma and Grandpa are Loureen's real parents. They already had her. And they decided to also adopt a son, me."

❄ ❄ ❄

After we got inside, Dad looked through the mail while I turned on the bathroom sink to put cold water on my hot face and red eyes. Not a bad day. Things turned out pretty good. They sure could have turned out worse. And I'd never had such a special moment with Dad. Now I knew why he yelled so much. He'd been adopted.

After cooling off, I went back into the kitchen to get a snack. Mom didn't seem to be around. Maybe she was shopping. That's probably why the school ended up calling Dad from work. They must have called the house first, and nobody had answered.

I suddenly remembered that I'd sent the ornament home ahead of me. Would I find it in the drawer like I had wished or would it pull some kind of mischief? No, how could it fool me this time? My words were clear and brief. There was no room for tricks. Still, I figured I should get to it quickly and make sure everything was all right.

I opened the bedroom door.

"Come in, Michael. I've been waiting for you."

I almost screamed. Another kid had gotten into my room. He was sitting at the desk examining the ornament. He hardly even looked up when I entered.

"Close the door," he said. "You don't want anyone to see us."

I know what you're thinking. You're wondering how some strange kid got into my room, some kid I'd never seen before. But believe it or not, the part about him getting in isn't what scared me. What scared me is that I *had* seen him before. The kid was me. I was staring at another Michael Owen.

"Dear God in heaven," I prayed out loud, "What has the ornament gone and done now?"

Chapter Eleven

The Other Kid

He even had the exact same set of clothes on.

"Who are you?" I shouted.

"That's a dumb question. Who do you think I am?"

"Well...You look like..."

"Go ahead and say it. I look like you. You feel like you're staring into a mirror. Don't you?"

"How did you get in?"

"The ornament sent me."

"Why? Nobody made a wish. I don't get it."

"You made the wish, Mike. You made it from Mrs. Harold's office."

"You know Mrs. Harold? "

"I know everyone you know...because I'm you."

"What did you say?"

"You heard me. I said I know everyone you know, because I'm you."

I pulled the ornament out of his hand. "You *are not* me!"

He laughed and sat down on the bed. "Don't you believe your own eyes?"

"You aren't me!" I said again, because I didn't know what else to say.

"Easy, Mike."

"You look like me. That's all. But you're not me. There's only one me!"

"You better quiet down or someone will hear us."

I sat next to him. "Get out of my room!"

"Don't you wanna know what's going on?"

I said nothing.

He went right on talking. "I'd be happy to explain if you'd just listen. You made a wish to send the ornament home before Mrs. Harold found it. The ornament can't do magic without the person who makes the wish. You were not in your bedroom, so the only way it could return to your room was to take you along."

"But it didn't take me along. I stayed in the office."

"Well...You did and you didn't."

"Huh?"

"I mean...Well, on one hand you're right. You stayed in the office. You needed to stay there. That was the whole purpose of the wish, for you to stay in the office looking like an innocent kid who had nothing in his pocket to hide. That's why the ornament had to leave you there. But the ornament also had to take you along, because, like I said, no magic can happen unless the person who makes the wish is in the same room."

"You're confusing me. You make it sound like the ornament left me behind and took me home at the same time."

He nodded. "Yes. That's it exactly."

"You're crazy!"

"Crazy? Come on, Mike. After all you've seen the ornament do? Can't you accept this too? The ornament split us into two people. There are now two Mike Owens, you and me."

"Now hold on. I'm the real Mike Owen. You're just some kind of copy."

"I could just as easily say that I'm the real one and you are the copy. Every experience you've ever had, I had too."

"Oh yeah?"

"Yeah!"

I just stared at him for a few seconds. "Prove it. Tell me something nobody else knows except me."

"Ok. You're in love with Renee."

I felt like my face was turning red.

"Gotcha," he laughed.

"Well...You're close. I like her. I don't love her."

"Not just you. Both of us. Only I don't mince words. Call it what you want. It's love."

"Well that proves you aren't me. You don't talk the way I do."

"You're partly right. In a way, I'm different now. The ornament made me a little more mature. Otherwise, we'd both be very confused. To help me understand what has happened, the ornament made me grow up a little."

"But you're the same size as me."

He pointed to his head. "I mean up here. The ornament made me grow a little, up here."

"Wait. What about the bad thing? At the office, the bad thing happened to Mrs. Harold. What was the bad thing here? For the ornament to work, two people have to be in the room, not one."

"The bad thing is happening to you right now. You're feeling upset because your individuality is being threatened. You don't want two Mike Owens in the world."

"But I wasn't in the room when you appeared."

"Well, you weren't but you were. Since we are the same person but also two different people, the ornament bestowed the bad thing upon you, an extension of me. You see, now that the ornament has helped me grow up, I don't mind having a duplicate. But since you do, the bad thing has happened to you."

I was so frightened and confused, I couldn't say anything. The new kid double put his hand on my shoulder. "Hey, cheer up. You know how the ornament can take bad things and make good things come out of them. We always wanted a brother, didn't we? Well, now we each have one. I'm like your twin brother."

"It's not the same. Twins are two different people, not the same person."

"Actually, that's not altogether true. Identical twins start out as the same cell. The cell later splits. Identical twins are separate people and the same person, just like us."

"It isn't like us!" I said.

"I suggest you lower your voice."

I whispered. "It isn't like us."

"Why not?"

"I don't know…Ah…Well, for one thing, twins don't split in the sixth grade."

"Well, yeah. You got me there. We are different in many ways. OK, we aren't *just like* twins. We're *similar* to twins."

"So you have all my memories? What happened just now out in the parking lot with Dad? What secret did he tell me?"

"Mike, try to follow what I'm saying. I don't know what happened after you sent me home. From that point on, our experiences have been different. In fact, I'd like you to tell me what happened from the moment I left the principal's office, till now."

We spent the rest of the afternoon talking. I actually started to cheer up after a while. I was surprised how fast I accepted the situation. I guess these last few days with the ornament had gotten me used to surprises and new adventures. It was like someone had opened a box of magic tricks and they just kept coming, each trick better than the one before. Every wish somehow got me into the kind of trouble that I could only get out of with another wish, and then that one got me in trouble and so on and so forth.

And now the trouble was explaining this to Mom and Dad.

"Maybe we could tell them you're a lost son," I offered.

"Oh, Mom had twins without knowing it, eh? Nice try."

"Well, how about a lost nephew? If we could get Aunt Loureen back here, she'd probably go along with it, pretend that she has a son she never told Dad about."

"Our parents aren't stupid. However, that is an excellent idea, at least the part about getting some kind of help from Aunt Loureen. So excellent, I already thought of it. While you were still at school and nobody else was home, I wrote her a letter. Things are getting too out of control. We need Aunt Loureen's wisdom. I wrote and asked her to come back as soon as possible. She has to start teaching her classes again soon so she should be back from England any time. And when she get's home, she'll find a letter waiting for her." He opened the drawer. "Here. Mail this tomorrow on your way to school. Remember, Aunt Loureen, with her charming stubbornness, hasn't entered the world of email yet."

He sure did talk grown up.

"Aren't you going to school?" I asked.

"Well we can't both go...At least not until there's a way to explain twin brothers. One of us can pretend to be sick while the other goes to school. If we play it smart, Mom will never figure it out."

"She'll write a note the next day for Mrs. Evans."

"Sure she will. And we'll tear it up because we won't need it."

"That will only work one or two times," I said. "We can't pretend to be sick forever."

"By then we'll think of something."

"Why should I be the one to go to school? Maybe I can take the day off tomorrow and you can go. I could use a day off after today."

"So could I. We both had the same day till an hour ago. Remember? Well, OK. I don't mind. I'll go. I'd like to see Renee anyway."

"Wait. No...I'll go...You can stay."

He smiled. "Sure, Mike. Whatever you say."

He *was* the more mature one. I could see that in a million ways. I didn't like the idea of him also loving Renee. I wasn't sure whether or not to be jealous. Could I be jealous of myself? Yeah...I could. He was so mature, he was really a different person. But to Renee, we would be the same person, so I guess there really wasn't any reason to feel jealous, but I still did.

He continued. "As for today, we must make sure that Mom, Dad and Shelly never see both of us together. The middle of the night is no problem. One of us can take the bed and one can sleep on the floor."

"Sure," I said. "Yeah, OK. We can flip a coin or something. But what about the rest of the time?"

"If one of us stays in the room at all times, we'll be OK. But when you hear someone coming, get under the bed or in the closet."

"How will you know it isn't me coming in?"

He thought for a second. "A secret knock. We'll knock twice, whichever one of us is outside."

"OK... I guess that plan is as good as any. Hey, what do I call you anyway? I feel weird calling you *Mike*."

"I understand. Too bad we don't have a middle name...How about *Sonny*? That's what Aunt Loureen always calls us. That name is just as familiar as *Mike*, but we'll also have different names."

I liked it. "OK...Sonny...Whew...Well, whose turn first? You wanna stay in the room or go out a while?"

"Oh you go for a while, by all means. I wandered around the house already before you got home. Speaking of which, I saw something interesting in Shelly's room, a rather unusual book."

"Book?"

"Yes, a book lying on her floor. I went in to examine her things because, as you'll recall, she was talking kind of funny yesterday, as though she were about to figure out the charm."

"Yeah...Hey, that's what I was gonna do, examine her room before she got home from school."

"I know. We both decided to do that when we were the same person. I ended up doing it first because I got home first. Anyway, she has a book. It's a very short book and I read it. You need to read it as well, twin brother."

"Why? What's up?"

"Let's just say that more happened with Shelly and the ornament yesterday than we were led to believe. We thought that her friends were the only ones who accidentally made wishes. Not so. Shelly made a wish too, and that book is the answer to her wish."

"Now wait a sec..."

"Just go, Mike. Go get it out of her room and read it. She'll be home soon.'

I hurried to Shelly's room and found the book instantly. She had a lot of books lying around, but it wasn't hard to guess which one my twin was referring to because one of the book covers showed a bright colored picture of our ornament with the castle in the glass. The title read: *The Magic Ornament of Lumas, by T.H Christian.*

Lumas...Lumas...That was the name of the country! The country Aunt Loureen mentioned! The name I couldn't remember! Inside this book must be the story of the ornament, where it came from, how it did magic, everything!

Chapter Twelve

The Book

Shelly bounced in, took one look at me, and started squealing. "You're not supposed ta be in my room!"

"Aww...Shut up and sit down! I wanna talk to you!"

"I'll tell Mom!"

"I just wanna talk! Where did you get this book?"

"I found it in the library."

"The school library?"

She nodded.

"But...But this is incredible. That's our ornament on the cover!"

"I know, silly. Why do you think I checked it out?"

"Were you looking for a book like this?"

"No. I was looking for *Horton Hatches The Egg*. But my teacher said we could only check out one book, so I picked this one instead 'cause I thought it might explain the magic charm Aunt Loureen told us about."

"Why are you so interested in that charm?"

What a stupid question. Why would a little girl not be interested in a magic charm? But I wanted to keep her talking so that I could maybe learn what had happened.

"'Cause I told the kids about it at Show and Tell. They asked me what the charm was."

"Yeah? Then what did you say?"

"I said I didn't know."

"That's it? Those were your exact words? Did you tell them you wished you *did* know? Anything like that?"

"Sure. Don't you also wanna know?"

That was it. So she *had* made a wish yesterday after all. As usual, I started thinking about the bad thing. Oh who cared! I was sick and tired of worrying about bad things. I decided not to even ask.

"Why didn't you tell me about this book?" I said.

"I forgot."

"Have you read it yet?"

"No, I can't. There are too many hard words. It must be for the bigger kids. But at first I thought it was for first graders 'cause it's thin and it has lots of pictures."

It did look like an easy book. And it did have many pictures inside, real cool pictures of castles, horsemen, dungeons, even angels. But when I glanced at the words, I could see it *was* a difficult book for little kids and not just them, I even noticed a few words I didn't know. I might need to use a dictionary if I wanted to understand it all.

"Will you read it to me, Mike?"

That would be the day, me explaining the secrets of the ornament to this little snip.

"Sure. Happy to. Let me go read it over myself first. Then I'll be able to do a better job of reading it you."

"I wanna hear it now."

"Well I'm not gonna read it to you now. I'm gonna read it over myself first, like I said."

"It's my book."

"It is not your book. It's the library's book. And you can get in trouble for checking out books that are for the bigger kids. You're lucky your teacher didn't notice."

Shelly looked like she was about to cry. I had gotten very good at lying.

"Hey, don't worry. I won't fink on you. Just...Hey, *Sesame Street* is on...Go watch that for a while and I'll read it to you later, OK?"

"OK," she said sniffing.

I went back to my room. "Sonny" wasn't in there. I figured he must be in the bathroom, 'cause I saw the door closed and the light on when I passed it in the hall. Now, from my room, I could hear him coming out.

"Michael? Where are you going?"

This was unreal. Mom was talking to Sonny on his way out of the bathroom, thinking he was me. Of course he *was* me, but not the real me or...well, you know what I mean.

"I'm just going back to my room," he said.

"Did you forget? This is your night to set the table."

Maybe having a twin around wouldn't be so bad after all...unless he ended up eating my dinner. Actually, I didn't care. I was too excited to eat.

As I flipped through the book, I started wondering how the ornament had gone about giving Shelly her wish. Was this book already in the library? Did the ornament just help Shelly find it? Or did the book magically appear on the shelf? And if it did magically appear, where did it come from? Some other country? Or maybe the ornament just made the book out of thin air. Maybe it existed only because Shelly got curious.

It sure looked like a regular book. It was old, with dust and stained pages. It also had a shelf number and one of those Library of Congress catalogue numbers. But I knew that didn't really mean anything because this was a clever ornament.

I turned to the first page and read the first sentence: "Many years ago in one of the other worlds God created..."

Hmm. The book mentioned God. Like I said before, our principal didn't believe in having religious stuff at school. Now, more than ever, I knew this book didn't really belong here. The ornament had snuck it in.

I continued reading. It seemed to be written as a children's fairy tale. Nobody would believe it for a second. They would think they were reading fiction. But maybe that style was just a trick from the ornament. Maybe the explanation of the charm was disguised as a fable. Well, I wasn't gonna be fooled. Since the charm was real, this story must also be real.

Many years ago in one of the other worlds God created, there lived a wise old ruler named King Crescent. King Crescent reigned over the country of Lumas, a most famous country, for in the land of Lumas it was always Christmastime. Since Christmas is God's special holiday, other worlds celebrate it too, but most of these worlds, like ours, celebrate Christmas only once a year. This was not so in the country of Lumas. King Crescent had observed that people were in their best moods and on their best behavior during Christmas season.

"If people could only be so well behaved all year long," the king said to his council of elders, "the world would be a better place. There would be no more war, because countries always hold truces during Christmastime and there would be no more poverty because people enjoy being generous around Christmastime."

And so the people of Lumas learned to celebrate Christmas constantly. Although they could not afford to exchange presents every day, they did leave the holly wreathes and lights on their houses. They also listened to Christmas music each and every day. Since this happened a long time ago, the lights were made of candles and the music was made from real instruments such as flutes or bagpipes.

What resulted, was the happiest, most friendly, most loving country the world had ever known. God Himself was so moved by their desire to celebrate Christmas eternally that He allowed it to snow all year round, not enough snow to bother people, just enough to enjoy.

"So that's why the ornament has that snow stuff inside," I said to myself. I continued reading.

On the other hand, the Kingdom of Baaman hated Christmas and had nothing to do with God. Although Baaman was a human king, the angel Lucifer kept him in power, whispering evil thoughts in his ear, thoughts which he believed were his own. These whispers encouraged all kinds of laws against any worship of God. Without God, the people of Baaman enjoyed misery and loved conflict. Children were never taught right from wrong. Crime was seldom punished, unless it was a crime against the king. Wars were waged with other kingdoms constantly. Darkness and thunder characterized Baaman's Kingdom just as color and snow symbolized Lumas.

The Kingdom of Baaman tried several times to wage war upon Lumas but God protected His people by surrounding the outskirts of the city with a blizzard so harsh that nobody could pass through it. Lucifer himself became very concerned about the peace and brotherhood of Lumas, for peaceful people ended up obeying God in the end, and that meant fewer souls for Lucifer to steal. Unable to conquer the country by using his human pawns, Lucifer instead dispatched Hamartio, one of his top angels, on a special mission. Like his leader, Hamartio was a wicked angel who had rebelled against God's goodness long ago. Hamartio was especially known for his cleverness and for his ability to trick people into doing wrong. His greatest trick was to make something go wrong with their lives in the hopes that they would blame God.

Lucifer bestowed extra special power upon Hamartio to assure a successful mission. Hamartio had the ability to make rich people lose their money. Hamartio had the ability to cause horses to buck the riders off their backs. Hamartio had the ability to make food sour, rooftops fall, arrows misfire, contracts disappear, agreements forgotten, anything which could cause arguments or fights. In no time at all, the people of Lumas changed from a peaceful nation to a nation of quarreling, feuding, and rioting.

But King Crescent was an insightful king. He knew this terrible turn of events had to have something to do with Lucifer, and he prayed that God would send an angel of His own to solve the problem.

God did hear the king's plea and gave the assignment to one of His favorite servants, the archangel Char. Char was a very handsome and very creative being. At times he was too creative. On many occasions he wanted to do things his way rather than God's way. Although Char would never dream of flatly disobeying God, he did argue with God a lot. God liked it when His angels had ideas of their own, but sometimes He knew that Char's ideas would not work. He would warn Char and occasionally forbid his plans if the plans were reckless and dangerous. But most of the time God did allow Char to try it his own way, just to teach him a lesson.

When Char heard about his old nemesis Hamartio, he got very excited and came up with a brilliant plan to stop him. God gave Char permission to try his plan, but he also left him with explicit instructions to stop right away if the plan was not working, return to heaven and discuss a new strategy with the other angels. Char agreed to do this, but secretly, he was positive his plan would work and he did not expect to return to heaven as a failure.

Char's plan was simple but effective. Every time Hamartio made something evil or sinister happen, Char found a way to turn it into a blessing.

If a person got sick from eating a food Hamartio had poisoned, Char would heal the person. When this happened, people gave God the glory and praise, which was proper because angels do not exist to take credit for themselves. Whenever a horse bucked his rider, Char would give the animal the ability to talk and understand human language. That way, the rider could explain how he felt about being bucked and could now have a new friendship with his horse. When people got into feuds due to Hamartio's tricks, Char would put special ideas into the minds of the opponents, so that they could figure out ways to end their disputes.

This plan did not restore Lumas to its earlier splendor and bliss. But it did provide balance, and certainly Char's influence was a great help.

Angels have the ability to make themselves invisible, even to other angels, so at first Hamartio did not understand why his evil magic kept turning into good. But in time, he figured out what was happening, so he sent a special message to Lucifer asking for power greater than Char's. Anticipating such a maneuver, God sent a message of his own, warning Char to return to heaven. Char was still so excited about his plan that he came close to disobeying God for the very first time in his life. "When Hamartio grows tired of his useless tricks and returns to the Kingdom of Lucifer, then God will see the wisdom of my plan." But instead of an outright refusal, Char sent word back to God, asking for an extension. This was a big mistake, for Lucifer had given Hamartio a power beyond imagination: *the ability to actually banish his opponent.* Angels are immortal and cannot die, but Hamartio was now able to do the next best thing: make a magic wish that Char would be locked up forever, unable to roam the streets and valleys of Lumas. The only limitation was that he could not send Char very far away. He would have to bind him somewhere nearby.

One Sunday afternoon, while resting after morning worship, King Crescent received word that a stranger had magically appeared in the castle's dungeon. Kings do not usually visit their own dungeons, but King Crescent made an exception that day. Looking through the bars on the door, the man identified himself as the angel Char who had been imprisoned for all time. At first the king was not sure what to make of the whole affair, for all he saw was a man, not an angel. But Char convinced him by performing miracles and granting wishes. He made gold appear. He made clothes change color. It seemed as though he could do anything, anything except let himself out of the dungeon. Of course the King immediately instructed his guards to release the prisoner, but the key wouldn't work. Crescent even ordered that the door be broken open with an ax Instead, the ax broke.

Char became a permanent guest of King Crescent. Although he could do miracles, his range was limited to that which affected the castle or people inside the castle. This did not help the citizens of Lumas because now Hamartio was free to raise havoc undisturbed. In time, the king allowed his subjects to visi Char at the castle and occasionally Char was able to make a sick person well again or a shrunken person large again. But this was a small consolation since Hamartio still had the ability to move around freely, all over the country.

Yet even now, on this terrible eve of darkness, something blessed came out of something evil, for King Crescent visited Char every day. They talked and got to know each other well. They discussed music, art and politics. They also played chess and they prayed to God together. They became such good friends that King Crescent began to pray constantly for Char's release. He made this petition not only on behalf of Char, but on behalf of his people who were being destroyed every day by the wicked angel. Crescent was an unselfish king. He knew that he was safe from evil inside the castle walls with his new angel friend, but his heart ached for the pain and suffering of his subjects. For some reason, the prayers were not answered. Char suggested that God, in all likelihood, was teaching him another lesson and that he should have returned to heaven when first ordered to do so. After hearing this, the king stopped praying and instead tried a bold new idea.

Lumas was famous for its special Christmas ornaments. People came from all over the world to buy them. Many of the ornaments were designed by the king himself and built by his personal craftsmen. One morning, Crescent visited Char in the dungeon and held up his latest creation. "It's a Christmas ornament, but look, see what's inside, a small replica of our castle."

Char liked the ornament but did not understand what Crescent had in mind. The king explained his plan. "You have the power to grant wishes. So does our enemy Hamartio. Your wishes cannot undo his, but you do have the ability to take them and rearrange them, to make something good come out of them. Hamartio wished that you would be imprisoned in this castle. Supposing you were to make yourself shrink to a size smaller than a seed and enter my brand new replicated castle instead? You would still be a prisoner and you would still be in the same castle, in a manner of speaking. Once inside the castle in the glass, we could quietly start passing the ornament around to our citizens, instructing them to make the kinds of wishes that will protect them from evil. Since our country is already filled with Christmas ornaments everywhere you look, the odds are, this particular ornament will stay camouflaged, escaping Hamartio's notice. In a hidden fashion you can be set loose outside these walls to shield our people again. You'll still be a prisoner, but you'll be freer than you are now, free to continue your miracles. It can be likened to a legal loophole."

Char was not sure how he felt about the plan, but by this time he had already been locked in the dungeon for months and he was willing to try anything. He said his farewells to the king, thanking him for being such a good friend in his time of need. Then he made a special wish (or more correctly put, a special prayer) that his sentence would be transferred from the real castle of Lumas to the replicated castle in the glass. The wish was granted and word began to spread amongst the people of Lumas that a new magic ornament was being circulated to help them overcome the wicked spells of the angel Hamartio.

Of course the new strategy only worked a short time, for Hamartio was an intelligent angel, not to be outdone by anyone. After he figured out that his enemy Char lived inside the ornament, he tried to destroy the ornament and force Char to return to the real castle. But Char had expected this attack and had made a special wish that the ornament could never be destroyed. Hamartio grew so frustrated that he finally decided to enter the ornament himself and kill Char personally. This was a foolish decision since Hamartio knew full well that angels cannot perish. He was not thinking because he made his choice in the heat of anger. But Char was ready. As soon as Hamartio entered the ornament, he made a wish that Hamartio could never leave. In many ways, this was a very noble sacrifice on the part of Char, for it meant that he would be battling his worst enemy for ever and ever, always fighting, never resting. But this decision limited Hamartio.

By now, the power of the ornament was common knowledge. It was also understood that somehow, Hamartio had gone away, although nobody knew quite how. King Crescent took possession of the ornament. Each and every day he granted an audience to those citizens with special requests. People would enter the presence of the ornament and make a wish for something pure or creative. Char would grant the wish, and then Hamartio would cause something evil to happen. Char would counter attack by re-channeling the power and causing the evil to find someone else, someone nearby who had not made the wish. He did not like seeing bad things happen to innocent people but his power was limited by the equal, yet evil, power of his opponent. This forced him to make less ideal, yet satisfactory decisions. Occasionally somebody would make a wish that he or she thought was good, but Char would perceive the wish as selfish or reckless, and refuse to grant it. At those times, Hamartio would grant the wish.

When people weren't making wishes, the angels were fighting. This went on year after year, decade after decade, until finally the angels' overwhelming passions melted together, transforming them into one single being, and the ornament took on a life of its own, a new hybrid personality, partly good, partly evil. This is the same kind of nature human beings have; partly good and partly evil.

Because the ornament could never be destroyed, it survived long after the Kingdom of Lumas faded into the annals of history. It got passed around from country to country as it changed owners over the years and still exists till this very day. But since its origins were in the Christmas country of Lumas, it only works outside of Lumas during Christmastime. God did send a prophet ages ago promising to someday separate the personalities so that Char could be himself again and Hamartio could receive the judgment he deserves. But it hasn't happened yet. Therefore children, should you stumble upon such an ornament, with a castle in the glass, remember, it is very much like yourself, a mixture of good and evil. Be careful, ever so careful about the wishes and choices you make.

I lay on my bed for hours thinking about the story. I even forgot about dinner and didn't care that Sonny must be eating in my place. Every ten minutes or so, I would read the short book again. It was the most unusual book I had ever seen. Most stories have endings. This one didn't. This one made me feel like the story was still going on, and I was a part of it. But then, it probably wasn't a real book anyway. It was probably what I'd guessed all along; an explanation, disguised as a book. I'll bet the author wasn't even a real person.

Did I believe the story? Well, I knew that in the olden days kings really lived in castles. As for angels, I'd learned about them in Sunday school. Of course, no angel in the Bible did this kind of stuff. Still, the Bible angels had a lot of power, like when they blew up those two cities, Sodom and some other place. The part about Lumas being in another world was the hardest to swallow. What did that mean anyway? Another planet or some magical hidden land somewhere on Earth? Or maybe neither. Many of my favorite science fiction TV shows talked about places called "other dimensions." I didn't know. But I did know what I'd seen the ornament do with my own eyes. I thought about those disappearing lima beans. Then I thought about lightning coming out of my fingertips earlier this morning. I thought about the big history question. And how about the weirdest miracle of all, a new twin brother? Yeah, I believed the story all right. Besides, it kind of explained the ornament's strange personality. It had seemed like the ornament was my friend one minute and my enemy the next.

I needed to talk with Aunt Loureen again. She had mentioned Lumas and King Crescent right from the start, before I even made that wish about her understanding the charm. Maybe the guy at the store who sold the ornament told her a little bit about the history, but still, that didn't explain why Aunt Loureen always talked about Christmas lasting all winter. Celebrating till March wasn't the same as celebrating all year round, but it was close enough to make Aunt Loureen seem as mysterious as the ornament itself.

Chapter Thirteen

An Argument About Shelly

It was late. Sonny had been the one to kiss Mom and Dad good night. I won the coin toss, so I got the bed and Sonny was going to sleep on the floor.

"So, how shall we go about explaining this to Shelly?" Sonny asked.

"To Shelly? What are you talking about?"

"She asked me if I would read the book to her tonight as though I had made her a promise. I assume that's something you said *you* would do."

"Yeah. Just to get her off my back. I wanted her to leave me alone while I read the book over myself."

"I figured as much. I told her I'd read her the book tomorrow."

"Good stall," I said. "But we can't keep stalling her forever. Maybe I can make up a fake story. You know, to kind of throw her off. I'll make up a good one...something as harmless as *Peter Rabbit*."

"No! No fake stories! We need to tell her the truth."

"Who says we do? Are you serious?"

Sonny nodded.

"No way, Sonny. I'm not explaining anything to that little brat."

"We have to, Mike."

"Why? Why do we have to?"

"Well, think about it. That book is here because the ornament answered Shelly's wish. That's the only reason we even have it. She wanted to know how the ornament works."

"She's a little baby. She can't handle stuff like this."

"Yeah? Like we've done such a great job."

"We did better than she would. She'll go around turning people into Barbie and Ken dolls."

"Stop exaggerating."

"I'm telling you, Sonny, it would be bad."

"You don't have to explain to me. She's my sister too."

"Then why would you wanna do something so stupid? What she doesn't know won't hurt her."

"The ornament wants her to know," he said. "Can't you see that?"

"No I can't. If the ornament wanted her to know, how come the book is written with words too hard for her to read?"

"So that one of us can read it to her and explain it to her. Otherwise the ornament wouldn't have led her to the book."

"Maybe the ornament just figured out a way to answer the wish without *really* answering it."

"That's ridiculous! The ornament could have simply chosen not to grant the wish at all if it was concerned about keeping things from Shelly."

"I don't know, Sonny. The book says there are two angels in there. Maybe the bad angel wanted to grant the wish and the good angel figured out a way to get around it."

"They aren't two angels any longer. They merged into one personality."

"Yeah, but the book said something about the personality being part good and part evil."

"The ornament still operates as a whole."

"What makes you so sure, Sonny?"

"The book said so."

"But don't you remember how we asked the ornament to control what Shelly wishes for?"

"Of course I remember."

"So this book is part of the control."

"It may very well be," he said. "But we can't ignore *our* role."

"We don't have a role!"

"Look, Mike, the ornament *did* grant the wish. That is the bottom line. It's a done deal and we need to quit second guessing the situation. The ornament gave Shelly the book, and if Shelly can't read the book herself, then the ornament intends for us to explain everything to her in ways a little girl can understand."

"Uh uh! Not me."

"Fine," Sonny said as he started to change into my other set of pajamas I had given him. "I'll do it then. I'm staying home tomorrow anyway, and Shelly will get back from school before you."

"That's not fair!"

"Who are you to say what's fair and what isn't? I'm telling her and there's nothing you can do to stop me."

"Sonny, you're making a mistake!"

"I don't think so. I'm the mature one, don't forget. The ornament made me that way for a reason. So if I think we should tell her, well then that's just what we're going to do."

"Oh, you think you're so smart!"

"Come on, Mike. Be reasonable. If we don't tell her, we're working against the ornament. Doesn't that sound kind of dangerous? Besides, explaining the ornament and giving her the ornament are two different things. We can still keep her from using the thing. We'll hide it."

"And she'll search the house...just like she was on an Easter egg hunt or something. I'm telling you, she'll find it, the little snoop!"

"That's less of a risk than working against the ornament!"

"Mike? What's going on in there?" The loud voice was coming from outside my bedroom door.

"Shoot! It's Dad." I gave Sonny a push. "Quick! Get under the bed!"

Dad opened the door, but Sonny got under in time.

"What's going on? Who were you talking to?" He glanced toward the closet. "Shelly, are you in here?"

"She's not in here, Dad. She's in bed. Honest."

"You sounded like you were talking to someone."

"That was just the radio. But see? I turned it off. Sorry I had it on so loud."

Dad stared at me for a sec. He had a very weird look on his face, like something else was on his mind besides me being too loud. I figured he must have still been thinking about our talk in the driveway. "Well, no more radio, Son. You need some sleep. You've had a big day."

After Dad left the room, Sonny squirmed out from under the bed.

"That was close," I said.

"Aw...No problem. Boy, he's changed. He hardly yelled or anything...Sounds like the two of you had a nice moment today. I want you to tell me more about it."

"I already told you."

"I'd like to hear more."

"What for?"

"Because he's my dad too, and that special moment was meant for me as much as it was meant for you."

Every time I thought I might start liking Sonny, he said something like this. I didn't want him to have my dad, and I didn't want him to have my girl. I just wanted him to go away.

Chapter Fourteen

Renee

Mom packed the ornament away in the attic, just like she said she would. She did it right before I headed out the door for school. Because of that whole day with Sonny, I forgot to make up a story about losing the ornament at school. But it didn't matter, 'cause as soon as she left to do some grocery shopping, Sonny snuck out of our room, climbed into the attic and fetched the ornament down. He didn't seem to be scared of the attic, like me. We figured that Mom would not have much reason for taking trips up to the attic to check on the ornament and we found a great place to hide it, at the bottom of my old army men box I hadn't used since I was a little kid.

Sonny did tell Shelly the story of Lumas and I have to admit, she took it well. Sonny ended up being right about that. Oh sure, hearing about the ornament thrilled her, but Sonny explained the rules carefully and Shelly seemed to understand. I guess being in on a secret with her brother (or brothers, as it was turning out to be) was exciting to Shelly and she wanted to do her part right.

It took her a while to get used to Sonny, but he somehow got her to accept even that. He was very good at talking. That's for sure. Shelly did spend a lot of time staring at the two of us together and asking a million questions. She even quizzed Sonny on events that only I would have known about to make sure he really was "another Mike." She also asked if the ornament could split *her* in two.

"I've always wanted a twin sister."

Two Shellys! That would be the day! I started getting irritated with her, but Sonny gently explained that we must be careful not to make those kinds wishes anymore, and I was surprised to see Shelly accept his warning. She didn't whine or plead or anything. Sonny seemed to know how to handle her in ways that I'd never figured out.

For the next couple of days we were able to confide in Shelly about everything. She even helped us distract Mom and Dad from ever seeing the two of us together. When one of us was eating dinner, Shelly would excuse herself early and sneak food into the bedroom to feed the other one.

Every day, Sonny and I took turns going to school. We couldn't pretend to be sick all the time. That only worked for a few days. Mom was usually home, so after a while we worked out a plan with Ben. His parents worked in the daytime, so he gave us a key to his house. Whichever twin didn't go to school, hung out there during the day. It was nice, because Ben had cable TV, a DVD player and lots of computer games.

Whichever one went to school filled the other in on what he'd missed. We even split the homework, which was totally cool. Sometimes I'd return to school the next day and some kid would mention something as if we had talked about it before, so there were a few close calls. But all in all, the trick worked. Since Ben and Cliffe were in on the secret, they helped to let me know about stuff that Sonny might have forgotten to tell me.

Joe Blankenship had been absent ever since the day of the big fight. I guess his parents were concerned or something. Anyway, I never ended up getting hassled any more by the principal, and the kids all treated me like I was some kind of new hero. At first I liked that, but after a while, I started feeling bad 'cause I knew I would never have been brave enough to fight Joe if it hadn't been for the ornament. Ben was brave without the ornament. I wondered why some people were brave and some weren't. I also wondered why I couldn't have been born as one of the brave ones.

Every day, Renee kept looking at me from across the classroom. She liked me all right, but I was still too scared to ever go up and talk to her during recess. That all changed one day when Sonny came home from school with some news.

"You did what?" I shouted at him.

"Take it easy, Mike. We talked. That's all."

"You talked to Renee?"

"Yes. In fact, I invited her to sit next to me during lunch. Is something wrong?"

"What did you go and do that for?"

"Because I like her. Why else would I do it? "

"Yeah? Well, it isn't fair! Renee is *my* girl!"

"*Your* girl? You can't even talk to her."

"Well, I met her first."

"And just exactly how do you figure that? We both met her at the same time."

"It's not fair, Sonny. Here you're talking to her while I'm stuck at Ben's house all day."

"So? Then the alternating day, you get to see her while I'm at Ben's. You can talk with her too, you know. Just because you're too scared, that isn't my fault."

"But now she'll think we're gonna talk again tomorrow, and I don't know what to say."

"Then I suggest you think of something."

"What did you guys talk about anyway?"

"All kinds of stuff."

"Well, tell me!"

"Oh gee...Let's see...We talked about other kids at school and our subjects. I asked her what she wants to be when she grows up. She wants to be a nurse."

"Yeah? Well, what else?"

"Her family moves a lot because her dad's in the Navy."

The next day Renee sat down next to me at lunch just like it was the natural thing to do. I was so scared, I could hardly even look at her. But I had to try. I wasn't gonna let Sonny steal my girl with his smooth words. It was hard to believe we were the same person, 'cause I felt jealous of him just like he was a different person.

"Hi, Mike."

"Hi, Renee. Ahh...Here, I saved you a seat."

"Thank you. I notice you always bring a bag lunch."

"Yeah. I don't like cafeteria food. But I guess you like it, huh?"

"It's all right. What are you doing your book report on?"

"*Tarzan*. How about you?"

"Oh, I'm doing *Anne of Green Gables*."

"That's cool. You know, the Tarzan in the books is different from the Tarzan in the movies."

"Oh? I didn't realize that."

Tarzan. Sheesh! What a stupid thing to talk about with a girl. She probably didn't care, but she was very polite and she acted like she *did* care.

"Yeah. The Tarzan in the books doesn't live in a tree or anything like that. He lives in Africa, sure, but it's in a house and he's real smart. He talks both English and French."

"I see."

I needed to get off of *Tarzan* fast, but I didn't know what else to say.

"That must be neat, having a dad in the Navy. My dad just works as an accountant."

"I wish my dad did something like that. Then we wouldn't have to move so much."

"Are you gonna move again?"

"Some day, probably. But I hope it isn't for a while."

"Yeah. That must be hard trying to make new friends all the time."

"It is. But it helps when I meet nice people...like you."

❄ ❄ ❄

I found myself whistling when I walked through the front door. My talk with Renee had gone well. I probably didn't do as well as Sonny, but I would learn.

When I walked into the living room, Shelly was sitting by herself on the couch crying. I ran over to her. "Hey! What's up?"

"Oh Mike! Something terrible has happened. Daddy took Caligula to the pound!"

Chapter Fifteen

After All, He's Only A Cat

I felt guilty because I had not paid much attention to Caligula lately. When I was at school I hardly ever thought about stuff at home. And then, even at home, Sonny seemed to spend more time with the cat than me. He had filled Caligula in on the new "twin" situation and he promised every day that we would keep him from the pound, except that we didn't. Still, the more I thought about it, the more I figured we might all be better off if Caligula just stayed where he was.

"Come in!"

Sonny had given me the secret bedroom door knock.

"Hi," he said coming in with a small bag of cheese puffs. Sonny plopped himself down on the bed. "I'm working on a plan to rescue Caligula."

"Rescue him?"

"From the pound."

"What for?"

"What do you mean 'what for?' Come on, Mike. We promised him we'd figure something out the day Mom gave us the news, back when we were one person."

"I know. And at first I was sorry to hear that Dad took him to the pound. But I've been thinking; that cat is out to get us, or at least one of us. He keeps threatening me with that wish."

"He's just frightened. Once we rescue him, he'll be so grateful, he'll abandon all plans of vengeance."

"I don't know, Sonny. I've never met a grateful cat. Mom's fed him for years. Does he ever thank her? No, he just sits there cleaning himself and acting like he owns the place. Besides, he sounded weird when he first threatened me. Caligula is getting scary. I say we leave well enough alone. Now that he's in the pound, he can't go near the ornament."

"But they'll kill him at the pound, Mike."

"Yeah? So? Then he *really* won't be able to make any more wishes."

"I don't understand you. How can you be so cruel? Especially when *I* don't feel that way at all. How can we really be the same person?"

"You're the one who keeps saying we're the same person, not me."

"Don't you care about anyone but yourself? That cat has been a part of the family for years."

"Oh sure he has...lying around sleeping all day. Dad's right about him. Good riddance."

"I don't think you really feel that way. I think you care about Caligula, but you're just too scared to try rescuing him."

"You're nuts!"

"You can't fool me. We're the same person. If I care about Caligula, so do you. It's just that I'm not as scared to act, because the ornament made me more mature."

"Would you shut up already about being more mature? If I hear that one more time..."

"All right...Never mind. Ok, let me just offer another reason to rescue Caligula."

"Yeah? What other reason?"

"The very thing you fear: if we don't help him, he might get even."

"How? He's nowhere near the ornament."

"I know. But if there's one thing we've learned about the ornament, it's that anything can happen. There could be unusual rules we don't know about yet, like the very reason the ornament split us. We weren't expecting that, were we? We didn't realize that to send the ornament home from school, the ornament would have to duplicate us first. Don't you think there could be other features which the ornament hasn't revealed yet? And remember, Caligula knows the ornament better than either of us."

"Better than you?"

"I just learned enough to make sense of our situation and I grew up a little, but that's nothing compared to Caligula. You made a wish that he would know everything, remember? He knows all the clauses and provisos. He may even know about the existence of another ornament somewhere with different abilities, or perhaps some other wishing device."

"That's stupid. He's at the pound. Where's he gonna find another ornament?"

"I'm just giving you examples. He may also know alternative ways to use the power of *this* ornament."

"Then why hasn't he already done it?"

"I don't know. All I'm saying is that anything is possible, including a hundred possibilities I haven't even thought of. We need to rescue him. We need him on our side. Otherwise, he's much too dangerous."

❄ ❄ ❄

Sonny was the one who called the meeting, but we were using Ben's house. Cliffe was gonna help us too, and even Shelly would be part of the plan, the big plan to rescue poor Caligula.

School was over for the day, and Mom said we could go over to Ben's house for a while. It was Tuesday afternoon. I was the last one to get there. I knocked on Ben's door.

"Come in," Ben said. "Everyone's waiting."

"Sorry it took so long," I said. "Mom saw Sonny leave with Shelly so she thought I already left. I had to lay low and wait for the right time."

"It's cool, " Ben said. "Hey, speaking of Sonny..."

"Yeah?"

"Don't get me wrong, Mike, but...Ah...I don't like him. I mean, I know he's supposed to be you..."

"He's not really me. He came from me. That's all."

"Well I'm glad to hear you say that. Because he *is* a lot different, and he seems to think he's in charge of this whole plan."

I shrugged. "Maybe he *should* be. The ornament did make him more mature."

"I know it did, and he won't stop reminding us. If you ask me, the ornament just made him more stuck up. I think we should all decide this thing together."

I realized right then that Ben was more mature than Sonny. Oh sure, Sonny used bigger words, but Ben was nicer and more friendly, and he acted that way without any help from the ornament. He also didn't go around pointing out how mature he was.

"OK, Ben...Sure. Whatever you think is best."

❄ ❄ ❄

Ben's parents weren't home, but Ben said they could come home any time, so we crowded into his bedroom. That way they wouldn't walk into the living room and hear us talking. Sonny called us to order just like he was in charge of a club or something. Once everyone shut up, Sonny began.

"OK. Let's add up what we have: a cat in the pound. And he'll be there only a few days. Then, after it's clear that nobody wants him, he'll be put to death."

Shelly started crying. I put my arm around her. "Don't worry. We won't let him die."

"Now then," Sonny continued. "Our purpose today is to figure out a way to get Caligula out of there."

Ben sighed. "That's fine, Sonny. I think we know this already."

"Doesn't hurt to review the situation. That way, we can better assess our position."

Ben gave me a look which seemed to say, "See what I mean?"

"So how do we get him out of there?" Cliffe asked.

"I'll make a wish!" Shelly said.

"You can't make a wish!" I snapped at her.

"I can wish as good as you!"

"That's not what I meant."

"What Mike means," Sonny started to say.

Ben interrupted him. "I think Mike can tell us for himself what he means."

Sonny looked surprised. "OK. Certainly. Go on, Mike."

"Shelly, none of us can undo this with a wish. I don't just mean you. I mean none of us. Once the ornament grants a wish, that's it."

"Then how do we get him out?" Shelly whimpered.

"Good question," Cliffe said. "Besides, even if we did get him out, wouldn't your dad just bring him back again?"

"You're right," I said. "He probably would. I didn't think of that."

Sonny still smiled. "Fortunately, I *did* think of that."

"There's a surprise," Ben muttered.

Sonny went on. "Don't forget, Aunt Loureen will be back soon. She must have received my letter by now."

"So your aunt is coming back," said Ben. "How's that gonna make a difference?"

"I just have a feeling that once Aunt Loureen returns, everything will be all right. All we have to do is keep Caligula safe until then."

"And when's she returning?" Ben asked. "Tomorrow? The next day?"

"Well, it's hard to be sure."

"I see. So you really don't know what you're talking about."

For a second, Sonny looked annoyed. But he tried to stay cheery. "My point is to take one step at a time. First we figure out a way to get the cat home. Then we figure out how to keep him there until Aunt Loureen returns. I assure you, she will not let Dad send him back to the pound."

"Whatever," said Ben.

Cliffe seemed very uptight. "If we can't use magic, what are we gonna do? We can't break the cat out of the pound. That's against the law. And we couldn't pull that off even if it wasn't against the law."

"Actually," said Sonny, "there may be a way for us to use magic after all."

"You guys said the ornament won't let you undo a wish."

"I know, Cliffe. But there might be a way to wish for something else and to have this something else benefit Caligula at the same time."

Ben shook his head. Cliffe was paying more attention. I wasn't sure what to think. It seemed hard to believe that a bunch of kids could outsmart some adults who worked at the pound, ornament or no ornament.

But Sonny still seemed as cheerful as could be. "Here's what we do. We go to the pound. Mike tells the people working at the pound that he wants to see his cat one more time. They let him."

"They let him?" Ben interrupted. "Who says they let him?"

"Why wouldn't they? And later, they see Mike leave. Only he won't really leave. They'll see me leave instead. Meanwhile Mike stays behind with Caligula."

I hadn't thought about fooling them with a look-alike. I had to admit, the plan wasn't bad so far.

"So," Sonny continued, "let's say Mike stays behind."

"Why me?"

"Or me. No problem. It can be either one of us. Let's say *I* stay behind."

"OK," Ben said. "We get it. They let you see the cat, maybe. You stay behind. Then what? You still have to get Caligula out of there."

"Right," Sonny said. "Anyway, I head inside and I pick Caligula up."

"Pick him up?" Ben said. "How will you even get into the cage?"

"The cages don't have locks because animals can't open cage doors and they don't need locks."

"You know that for a fact?"

"I'm assuming."

"Oh...Great."

"Trust me, Ben. OK. If they have locks, I'll figure out a way to get in. I'll ask if I can hold the cat and pet him."

"Then what?" I asked.

"Then I'll make a wish, but I won't wish about Caligula. I'll wish about myself. I'll wish for the ornament to magically transport me home, just like it did before when it sent itself home from the principal's office."

"But we can't use wishes."

"No, Mike. That is not so. We *can* use wishes. We just can't wish Caligula home. That's all. But if I'm holding Caligula while I make the wish and if I also wish that everything I'm holding goes home with me, Caligula and I might both disappear in the wink of an eye."

"That's it?" said Ben. "That's the big plan?"

"Sonny," I said, "you can't trick the ornament. The ornament won't let u undo the wish."

"Mike, it isn't a matter of tricking the ornament. Like you said, the ornament has a good and an evil side. The evil side wants to keep Caligula in the pound. What we do, is give the good side, the side that used to be the angel Char, a chance to help get around that wish."

"You said the ornament works as a whole."

"It does. But think...Char must be struggling to come out and be himself again. We'll be helping him with his struggle, giving him something to fight for."

"How can he fight if he isn't alive anymore?"

"He's still alive. The good part of the ornament is all that's left of him. But that's still a kind of existence."

"Yeah? Well that's what I was trying to say the other night and you shot me down. Now just to back up your plan, you talk differently about Char."

"I'm sorry you're having trouble understanding..."

"Don't start telling me that the only reason I can't understand is because you're more mature. I'm just as smart as you are."

"Smarter, if you ask me," Ben said.

Sonny tried to stay calm. "Who said anything about being smarter? The ornament just gave me some extra information."

"So you know all this for a fact?" I asked.

"No, he doesn't." Ben said. "He's assuming again. Right, Sonny?"

"I feel optimistic," Sonny answered.

"Oh yeah?" Ben said. "So when you transport home, what then? Will the ornament make another copy? Will we have three of you after this?"

"Of course not," Sonny laughed. "The ornament only did that before because I, that is Mike and I, had wished that the ornament *itself* would transport home. The ornament was unable to go home and leave me behind at the same time. But now, since I will be wishing that I go home with the ornament, such duplication will be unnecessary. And Caligula will be going home with me, so he can serve as the second person in both places."

"But then something bad will just happen to Caligula all over again," I reminded him.

"One step at a time, Mike. Remember, all we have to do is keep him alive till Aunt Loureen comes home."

"I think the plan has a lot of problems," Ben said.

"Me too," Cliffe added.

"I like it," Shelly said.

Sonny shrugged. "I'm open to suggestions if anyone has a better idea."

Ben started tossing his baseball into the air. "I'm not sure any idea will work."

"Then why not try *my* idea?" Sonny said with a cheerful shrug.

I stood up and looked out the window. "It might work, if we could get one of us in there to make the wish without being seen."

Sonny agreed. "That is the hardest part. That's where us working as twins becomes an advantage. And that's why we all need to go together. Here's what we do. After school, we all ride our bikes to the pound. I'll ride our old bike. Mike, you can ride the new one. And you all go in without me. I stay outside. Mike, you tell them that Caligula is your cat, that you just want to say goodbye to him. They take you to his cage and the rest of you ask if you can hang around and look at other animals. Stay together as a group. Then, I'll kind of mosey inside. If the rest of you crowd around me, they might not notice that there are two of us. You go in, see? You ask the caretaker if you can have a moment alone with Caligula. The caretaker leaves. At the right time, I approach the caretaker, tell him I'm ready to go home. He thinks I left Caligula back in the cage. I leave with the other kids. Meanwhile, you pick up Caligula and quickly make the wish."

Ben shook his head. "And when he discovers a missing cat, he won't suspect Mike?"

"Maybe. But he will have seen Mike leave without the cat. And what if he *does* suspect? So what? After all, Caligula is just an animal. It's not like they're going to call a detective. Why put so much effort into finding a creature of whom they were just going to put to sleep anyway?"

"Only one problem," I reminded him. "First you said *you* were going to the cage. Now, you switched it back to me again."

"Which one of us does what is not the point, Mike. However, I do suggest that you go into the cage. The more I think this through, the more I feel that's the better idea."

"How come?"

"Because once you're there with the ornament, you can disappear and get out quickly. If they should find the cat gone before the rest of us leave, if they should start interrogating us, then I am the better one to have around because I..."

"Because you are the mature one," Ben finished with a frown.

"Exactly, Ben."

"Sonny, what if they won't let me see Caligula? What if they want me to be with an adult or something?"

"They just might. That's why we bring Shelly along."

"Me?"

Sonny kneeled down next to her. "You have a very important part, little sister. If they won't let you and Mike in to see Caligula, you start bawling. They'll never resist a little girl bawling her eyes out."

Shelly laughed.

"So, Shelly and I are going in together? "

"Yes, Mike, at first. Then you send Shelly out to join the rest of us. Tell the caretaker it's too rough on her seeing Caligula about to die and all. In fact, that will play out perfectly, because you need to be alone with Caligula anyway. This gives the caretaker a reason to leave you alone for a second."

"It just might work," Cliffe said. "What do you think, Ben?"

"I don't know." He paused for a sec and then added, "I guess we can give it a shot."

Shelly raised her hand.

Sonny laughed. "Shelly, this isn't school. You don't have to raise your hand."

"Well, I got a question."

"Go on. What's your question?"

"How's the ornament gonna work any more? I haven't seen Christmas lights up for days."

The rest of us stared at each other. Nobody said anything 'cause we all felt so stupid. How could we have forgotten?

Even Sonny wasn't smiling anymore. "No more lights, you say?"

"There was one house that still had them in our neighborhood, but last night Mom and I drove by after my Brownies meeting and those lights weren't on any more either."

Chapter Sixteen

A Sweet Little Girl

I heard about this next part of the story from Sonny. I wasn't there myself. He and Shelly went to visit the last house in the neighborhood with its Christmas lights up. The lights had been turned off a few nights ago, but Sonny figured if they kept them as long as they did, he might just be able to talk them into turning them on again.

He brought Shelly along for the same reason he wanted her at the pound. Sonny had it in his mind that grown ups could never resist cute little kids. He was probably right. Shelly never seemed all that cute to me, but I could see that grown ups did look at her that way. Besides, Sonny had been right about everything else up to now. He sure was right about explaining the ornament to Shelly. If not for her, we all would have forgotten about the Christmas lights. We would have tried our rescue with an ornament that didn't even work anymore.

"There it is," Shelly said. "Look, Sonny. The lights are still on the house. Won't the ornament work as long as the lights stay up?"

"No, Sis. Lots of people leave them on the house so that next year they don't have to put them up again. But the ornament only works if the lights are actually turned on."

"But they were never turned on in the daytime anyway. And lots of wishes came true in the daytime before. How come?"

"I'm not sure. The ornament is very mysterious. It probably has something to do with the spirit of Christmas, the intentions of people to turn them on each night...Something like that. Remember, the citizens of Lumas celebrated Christmas with their hearts as well as their decorations. OK. Here we go."

"Can I ring the bell?"

"Sure. Go ahead."

An older, kind looking lady opened the door. "Yes children. What can I do for you?"

Sonny poured on the charm. "Excuse us for bothering you, ma'am..."

"Oh, not at all."

"I'm Mike Owen," Sonny said. "This is my sister Shelly. We live around the corner on Minas Drive."

"Well hello there, Shelly! What a pretty little girl you are!"

Shelly didn't say anything till Sonny poked her. Then, with a fake smile she said, "Thank you."

"Anyway," Sonny continued, "we couldn't help but notice the beautiful Christmas lights on your house."

"Oh, how thoughtful of you to tell me. Christmas is such a wonderful season. Is it not?"

"Yes indeed, ma'am. A joyous time of the year to be sure. And it meant so much to us when you kept your lights up long after Christmas ended."

"I do enjoy leaving them up for a while. I would probably keep them up even longer if I could afford it. But I'm afraid it makes up quite an electric bill."

"Oh I can understand that, ma'am. I certainly can. The cost of living is always a challenge."

"Shelly dear, how would you like a piece of candy?"

"Sure!"

"Come in, both of you...Please."

The lady brought them into her dining room. Shelly got excited when she saw a big cuckoo clock on the wall.

"Oh, I'm so glad the two of you dropped by." She pulled out one of those nice Christmas candy boxes, the kind that were wrapped like presents, filled with small bite sized chocolates on small fan shaped pieces of paper. "Here, have piece, both of you. Take as many as you want."

"Thank you, ma'am," Sonny said as he reached for a light colored chocolate.

"I wanted that one!" Shelly blurted out.

Sonny gave it to her. He needed to keep Shelly in a good mood, and she was about to ruin everything.

"I don't get many visitors, children. I do hope you'll feel free to stop by any time you want."

"Thank you, ma'am. That's very considerate of you. Actually, as a matter of fact, Shelly and I were hoping to bring some friends by tonight."

"Tonight, you say?"

"Yes. We wanted them to see your lovely Christmas lights."

Sonny sure knew his words, and he knew old ladies enjoy words like *lovely*.

"Oh dear," she said. "I wasn't going to be home tonight. Our church is having a potluck."

"Well, we don't need to come in, ma'am. We just wanted our friends to *see* your lights."

Actually, nobody even needed to *see* them. All that needed to happen was for the lights to be on. Sonny knew that if she agreed to turn them on tonight, we could all head for the pound today. And if he could talk her into turning them on even longer, we could have a few more extra wishes to use, should we need them.

"I know its expensive, ma'am, but they really do keep the spirit of Christmas fresh and alive, and I had hoped we could prevail upon you to turn them on for a few more days or so."

"Well, my son-in-law was going to take them down tomorrow."

Sonny gave Shelly his special look which was actually a signal that they had agreed on before.

"Oh please, ma'am," Shelly said on cue. "I was so sad when I didn't see the lights any more. Please don't let him take them down. Not yet!"

"There there. Come here, child. Sit right down here on my lap. Such a little doll. Why of course I'll leave them up for a while."

Sonny tapped her shoulder. "What do you say, Shelly?"

"Thank you, ma'am."

"It's my pleasure, Shelly."

"Can I have some more candy?"

Sonny blushed. "I think we've had enough, Sis."

"Oh nonsense! She can take as many as she likes, the little dear. And you… You are a very well mannered young man."

"That's very kind of you to say so."

As soon as they got back outside, Sonny gave Shelly a big hug. "Good job. Better hide those candies. Don't let Mom see them."

"That was fun!"

"I'm glad you enjoyed yourself, because you have to do the same thing at the pound. You're a sweet little girl. You need to lay it on thick. OK?"

"Sure! I like you, Sonny. I have fun with you! I like you better than Mike!"

Yeah, that's right. Sonny went out of his way to share Shelly's comment with me. Otherwise I wouldn't have been able to write it down and tell you about it. Maybe Ben was right. Maybe Sonny wasn't so mature after all. Bragging sure didn't seem mature to me. Besides, it hurt my feelings. Still, I could see why Shelly made the comment. Sonny treated her nicer than me and spent more time with her. If I had been there, I would have socked her the minute we got out of the house. I would have said something like, "What's the matter with you, asking for more candy like a greedy, little pig?"

But Sonny hadn't socked her. Instead, he hugged her. I saw Shelly as a brat. Sonny liked having a little sister.

Chapter Seventeen

The Rescue

"Can I help you?"

We were there at the pound, all of us; me, Shelly, Cliffe and Ben. Sonny was waiting outside, just like we had planned. The man behind the counter seemed kind of mean. It was hard for me to speak. I still think Sonny would have been better for this part.

"Yeah...Ah...We wanna see our cat."

"Your cat?" He looked like was ready to bounce us out the door. "Now what are you kids doing here?"

"Our cat is here in the pound."

"He's black and white," Shelly said. "He looks just like Sylvester from the

Tweety Pie cartoon."

I could see that Shelly was not making a cute impression on this man like she did with the old lady.

"How did your cat end up in the pound?"

"Our dad brought him," I said.

"You mean he's not here by mistake? Your dad wanted to get rid of the cat?"

"Yeah."

"So you're not here to claim him, then."

"No, sir. We just wanted to visit. So we could say goodbye."

"Now, son, do your parents know you're here?"

"Yeah," I lied. "They said we could come...You know...So we could say goodbye and all."

"Sorry, son. Can't do it."

I glanced at Shelly, giving her the signal to start crying. If she didn't lay it on thick, this whole thing would be over before it even got started. Probably her crying wouldn't work on this guy, but there was a lady doing some work in the back part of the room. If Shelly was loud enough, maybe we could catch her attention.

Ben tried to help. "Can't they just say goodbye, mister?"

"Look, kids, we aren't running a zoo here. This isn't a place where people visit animals. Maybe if you were accompanied by some adults, it would be different."

Shelly started in. "Now I'll never see our poor cat again. I never even got to say goodbye."

I put my arm around Shelly. Cliffe started to take out a hanky for her, but Ben shook his head. Ben was smart enough to know that if we went overboard, nobody would buy the act.

"Sorry, kids. Like I say, if you want to come back with your folks, we can work something out."

"What's wrong?"

Good! It was the woman worker. She would soften for sure because women always soften easier than men.

"What's the matter with the little girl?"

"Aw...They have some cat in here. Their dad brought him in."

"His name is Caligula," Shelly cried. "He's the sweetest cat in the world and

114

we just wanted to say goodbye, and he won't let us."

The woman bent low and gave Shelly a hug. "It's OK, sweetie. There's nothing to get upset about...Griff, why can't they go back there for a minute?"

"They're kids!"

"So? Take them back to see the cat! It isn't going to hurt anyone."

The man shook his head. "Oh, all right." He asked for an address and looked through a file. Finally he pulled out a card.

"Don't you have computers?" Cliffe asked.

"Shut up!" Ben said.

"OK, kids. Let's go see the cat. But just for a minute."

"We'll wait for you out here," Ben said.

"You can all go," the woman smiled. "We don't mind."

"Ah...We wanna stay out here," Ben said. "We have some questions."

"Questions? Why certainly...All right...Well, Griff can take your friends. I'll stay out here and answer your questions."

Shelly and I were led down a hallway. I could hear them talking as we walked out of the room.

"What kinds of questions do you have?"

"My friend Cliffe here wanted to ask you something about the pound."

"Go ahead, young man. What's your question?"

"Ah...Ah...Do you ever keep alligators here?"

I didn't hear the rest. Alligators! Sheesh! What a granite head!

We were led through a whole mess of cages with dogs and cats inside. Sonny was right. The cages didn't have locks. Sonny was always right. Caligula was in a big cage with two other cats. I wondered what it would be like with him talking to me in front of them. But then I remembered, because of my wish, I was the only one who could hear Caligula speak English, so the most we would get out of the other cats were some curious stares. Actually, Caligula looked very happy to see us.

"There you go, kids. I assume that's him, the one who looks like Sylvester."

"I can't stand to look at him," Shelly said just as Sonny had instructed her.

"But you wanted to see your cat. That's what you said."

"I know, mister. But I think she's upset 'cause she knows he's gonna get killed."

"Mike, please! Can we go?"

"I wanna sit with him for a sec, mister. Would you mind taking her back out to my friends?"

At first he just looked at me, like he was ready to bawl me out or something. But then he went ahead and nodded. "Yeah, OK. Stay away from the other cages. I'll be back in one minute."

Meanwhile, Ben had asked the woman in the outer office for some information about pounds. He said it was for a report in school. She went into a back room to look for a brochure. Sonny snuck in and crouched behind a chair. Then Shelly and the man returned right away.

"What's wrong?" Cliffe asked, pretending not to know anything.

"She got kind of scared when she saw the cat in the cage. Here, little girl... Wait here with your friends. I'll go get your brother."

Sonny popped out from behind the chair. "I'm all finished, mister."

The man was quite startled. "Oh. Hmm...Said goodbye already, did you?"

"Yes. Thank you for the opportunity. It was most kind of you."

The woman returned to the counter. "Here you go, kids. Here's one of our brochures."

After they got outside, Ben jabbed Sonny with his elbow. "What's the matter with you, talking so weird?"

"What do you mean?"

"'Thank you for the opportunity. It was most kind of you.' Can't you just act like a normal person? Couldn't you have at least tried to sound more like Mike?"

"What difference does it make? It worked!"

"How did you get in?" Caligula said to me.

"I don't have time to explain. I worked with Sonny."

"Oh, I get it. Some of that twin trickery?"

"Yeah. Anyway, I came to get you out of here."

"Well it's about time. Tomorrow is D-Day."

"I know. Sorry. It took us a while to come up with a plan."

"Did it really? I'll bet if the pound put humans to sleep, people would have

116

come up with a plan long ago." All of a sudden, his eyes looked wide and sneaky. "You brought the ornament along, didn't you?"

"Maybe I did, maybe I didn't."

"It's in your pocket."

"How do you know?"

"I'm a cat. Cats..."

"Yeah yeah...Cats sense these things."

"That's right. We do."

I noticed the other cats looking at us very strangely. This was all so weird.

"In any event," Caligula continued, "you're very predictable. It doesn't take a rocket scientist to figure you out. You always keep the ornament in your pocket when you have some new harebrained scheme. The kid gunslinger, fastest ornament in the west!"

"Yeah? So? How else am I suppose' ta hide it?"

"Interesting situation. Once again I find myself in the same room as the ornament. What makes you think I won't make my wish? I've been planning it for quite some time. I've thought it through very carefully."

"You won't make any wishes."

"I won't? Why won't I?"

"Because you need me to get you out of here."

"Perhaps. Assuming you succeed. So far, your track record hasn't been very good."

"I got in, didn't I?"

"Ok. Well, let's hear it. Tell me the plan."

"I'm gonna make a wish that the ornament sends us both home."

He shook his head. "You haven't learned a thing, have you?"

"It worked before. I sent the ornament home from school."

"First of all, even if it worked, your dad would simply pick me up, plop me into another portable cage and drive me to the pound all over again...Or maybe just shoot me himself. Second of all, you cannot undo a wish with another wish. You have to try human effort, something non-magical. I've told you that before. If I thought we could undo things I'd just wish myself out of here right now and leave you behind."

"I know we can't make another wish about *you* and the pound. But I won't

117

be wishing about you. I'll be just wishing that *I* can magically disappear and reappear at home. But I'll hold on to you while I do it. See the difference?"

"Three days and this is what you came up with?"

"We can at least try."

"It's the lamest, stupidest plan I ever heard."

"Oh just shut up! I'm gonna give it a try."

He sighed. "Yeah...Sure...Go ahead. Get it over with."

I picked him up. "I wish that I can be sent home, magically, me and everything I'm holding."

Nothing happened.

"Golly," said Caligula. "It didn't seem to work. Gee, imagine that." He jumped out of my arms and back down to the floor.

I felt so dumb, I couldn't even look him in the eyes. "I don't know what to do. We all thought..."

"Oh, you all thought. You and your idiot friends all thought...Well, here's what I think. I think I'm doomed. I think I'm finished. I think tomorrow is my last day alive and I think I have you to thank."

I started to open up the cage so that I could scoot out of the way fast, but there wasn't enough time.

"Where do you think you're going, kid? You don't get off so easily."

"You're not really gonna make a wish."

"Oh? Just watch me."

I pushed the door open and darted out, but I could hear his wish. He made it fast and loud.

"Ornament, I wish that Renee will move."

"No!"

"That's right, ornament, Renee, Mike's Renee, the Renee he's in love with. Have her dad transferred again at work. Move her to another city or even another state."

"Stop it! Please stop!"

"I'm done."

I was crying. "Why did you do that? I came to help!"

I don't think I'd ever felt so awful.

"It could have been worse, kid. Consider that. It could have been much

118

worse. I didn't wish you any harm, no real harm anyway. We cats are more civilized than you think. We have standards even where revenge is concerned."

"I would have rather been sick. I would have rather been dead."

"Well, don't go wishing it. One never knows what that fickle ornament may do."

"A lot you care!"

"I do care. I don't want you harmed. I never really did. I was much more cautious than *you've* ever been. I figured out a way to teach you a lesson without doing any serious, irreparable damage. You're far too young to be in love anyway. Nothing would have come of this. In time, you'll meet someone else. But yes, it hurts you now, temporarily. That was my intention. It's good for me and bad for you at the same time. And yet, as I said, not incredibly bad. You pay, but you don't get destroyed in any substantial manner."

I just stared at the floor. He continued. "You may feel right now like you'd rather be dead. But everybody who falls in love feels that way. It would have happened sooner or later. I just rushed the process. That's all I did. And in time, your bad feelings will pass. They always pass."

"You're the meanest creature I've ever known!"

"Mean, am I? Considering that I'm about to die, I could certainly have been far more vindictive."

"Hey! How did you get in?" The caretaker had heard me yelling. I was so upset, I had forgotten to be quiet. "Now, son," he said. "I've been very patient with you. But there's no place for sneaks around here. You better go on home before I call your parents."

I walked out of the room and I didn't look back. I didn't care anymore what happened to Caligula. Let them kill him. He deserved it.

Chapter Eighteen

The Most Terrible Wish Of All

It was late in the afternoon. Mom and Dad were gone. They took Shelly to the store for some new shoes. Sonny and I were in the living room.

"Great plan," I said. "Real great plan."

"I thought it would work."

"Yeah? Well it didn't! Guess you aren't as mature as you thought."

"It has nothing to do with maturity. Sometimes plans don't work out. You need to learn that."

"Oh, I need to learn that? When? When I'm as big as you? You're big, all right. You're a big blowhard! And now, thanks to that stupid plan, Renee is gonna move." I quieted down. Thinking of Renee made me do that. "Or *is* she gonna move? Do you think maybe this will be one of those wishes that the ornament says 'no' to?"

"Don't count on it."

121

"But it could happen that way."

"I don't think so. Caligula knows all about the ornament because of your previous wish. He knew what he could wish for and what he couldn't wish for. He knew it far ahead of time. It'll happen, all right. Tomorrow, at school, Renee will tell the others that she's moving some place far away."

"Well, that's your fault!"

"Mine?"

"For putting Caligula close to the ornament. I warned you!"

"Have it your way. I'm gonna read now."

"How can you think of reading at a time like this?"

"Reading relaxes me. Besides, it's an assignment for tomorrow."

"That's OK," I said. " I'll go to school."

"No, you won't. It's my turn."

"I know. But I wanna see Renee before she goes."

Sonny opened up his school book and answered me without even looking up. "I'm sure it will be a few weeks or months before she actually moves. You'll have plenty of time."

"We don't know that. With the ornament's power, she could leave at any time, and I wanna make sure I see her."

"So do I," Sonny said.

"Why do you need to see her?"

Sonny put the book down. "You're joking, right? My purpose is the same as yours, to tell her that I like her, to get her new address, so we can write. Stop looking at me like that. We both feel the same way about Renee. We've been through his before."

"Well, I knew her first, and I liked her before you were even born."

"I was born the same day as you, Mike."

"You were born last week from the ornament."

"We've been through that before too. Quit acting like you're the true Mike Owen."

I walked right up to his face. "I *am* the true Mike Owen. You're nothing like me!"

"Only because the ornament made me more mature. And speaking of maturity, it's the best argument for letting me handle the Renee situation."

"What do you mean?"

"I mean I can talk to her. I can tell her how I feel. What are you gonna do? You're so shy you can hardly breathe around Renee. You'll mumble, bumble, and stumble your way through and you'll never end up saying a thing."

"Oh, you're such a big shot with all of those fancy words. You only talk that way because of the ornament. Well, maybe I'll make a wish that *I* can be mature too."

"Don't go making any more wishes," Sonny said. "You just keep getting yourself in trouble. Besides, the ornament is not going to change your personality."

"Oh yeah? It changed yours."

"Only because it had to, so that we could make sense of the predicament."

"So who says it can't happen again? Maybe I'll just try anyway."

"Oh, you'll try, huh? Shall we review the results of your tries? You have a cat in the pound. You almost killed Joe Blankenship."

"Me? I almost killed him? We both did that, Sonny! If we're really one person then we both did it!"

"We *were* the same person. Now we're two different people. Yes, I did those things. But I've changed. I've grown up. And frankly, I'm the one who deserves Renee, not you."

That was the last straw. I jumped on top of him. We both rolled over on the floor. Sonny may have been more grown up in the head, but his body was the exact same size as mine so it wasn't hard to knock him over.

"Get off me! Mike, I'm warning you...Get off me!"

"I hate you! I wish you'd go away and never come back!"

We both froze instantly, because the ornament was still in my pocket and we realized at the same time what had happened. I got off him fast.

"I'm sorry, Sonny. I didn't mean that. I didn't mean it as a real wish. It just slipped out."

"I know," he said gently.

"I'll take it back. Ornament, I didn't mean that wish."

Sonny just shook his head. "Don't bother, Mike. You're too late."

"It's not too late!"

"Yes it is."

"But you're still here. So we must still have a chance."

"You can't undo a wish that's already been made. I can feel the power of the ornament surging through me."

"You can? What's happening?"

He still sounded calm. "I'm going away, like you wished. That's what's happening."

"I didn't mean it, Sonny!"

"I know you didn't, Mike. You were angry and you weren't thinking. You used careless, thoughtless words, just like Aunt Loureen always warned us about. It's all right. I spoke carelessly myself. I shouldn't have said that I deserved Renee more than you."

"There must be something we can do."

"We can say goodbye. I'm sorry you didn't like having me around. For what it's worth, I *do* like you. It was nice having a brother, even if only for a few days."

Then he disappeared right in front of my eyes. For a few seconds I just stood there, staring at where he had been. Where did the ornament send him? Was he back inside of me? Had we joined together again? It didn't seem like it. Wouldn't I feel something? Sonny had felt the ornament's power. Why didn't I feel anything? Probably because we hadn't rejoined. But then, I didn't feel anything the day we split either, so I really didn't know. But if he were part of me again, that would mean the original wish that split us had been undone and that couldn't be. So something else had happened to Sonny. Maybe the ornament just made him disappear. Maybe he was dead. What had I gone and done with my big, stupid mouth? All I could think about was how forgiving he sounded. Sonny, my mature self, the "me" I might have become when I grew older. That's when it hit me. Sonny was right. We were really like brothers. He was the older brother I'd never had. Fine time to realize it. Now he was gone, and I would never see him again.

There was a knock on the door. I felt so scared, I just sat there without doing anything.

"Nephew! Nephew, are you in there?"

"Aunt Loureen!" I ran to the front door, popped it open and ran into her arms crying, kind of like that day I cried in Dad's arms.

"What is it, Sonny? What's wrong?"

I could barely talk over the sobs. "I'm not Sonny. Sonny is dead. Sonny is dead and I killed him!"

Chapter Nineteen

The Return of Aunt Loureen

I spent the rest of the afternoon talking and filling Aunt Loureen in on all that had happened. Sonny had told her a lot already in the letter, at least the part about us splitting into two people. Whenever I started to get upset, she dried my tears and gently kissed my forehead. She also kept telling me that Sonny wasn't really dead. When I asked her how she knew, she just said, "Trust me, Nephew." She also went out of her way to call me *Nephew* instead of *Sonny*. She'd called me that before, but she'd always called me *Sonny* more and right now, she knew that it would make me feel bad to be called by that name.

We talked about all kinds of other stuff too, especially the book. I had looked forward to this. I had wanted to know why Aunt Loureen knew some of the things which the book talked about.

"Somehow the store owner knew about a kingdom called *Lumas* and its ruler *Crescent*. He really didn't know anything else, or at least he pretended not to. I might not have believed all his claims about a charm but the familiarity and my inability to recall where I'd heard of the ornament before...well that was such a mysterious feeling, I just had to buy it."

"Are you sure you never read the book as a kid?" I asked her. "Or did your mom maybe read it to you?"

"No. I never knew this book," she said thumbing her fingers through the pages and glancing at the pictures. "But, as I said, when that storekeeper mentioned the word *Lumas* and talked about King Crescent, it sounded familiar."

"How could it be familiar if you didn't already know the story?"

"Good question. At the time, I just trusted my instincts. Intuition suggested that I buy the ornament, even though I didn't understand its familiarity. But I can tell you now what was happening because the truth has become crystal clear. It had to do with your very first wish."

"You mean where I wished you would understand the charm?"

"Yes, exactly. Obviously, I could never understand the power of the ornament if I did not first find it and purchase it."

"Huh?"

"I mean to say that a large part of your wish coming true was for us to take possession of the ornament in the first place."

"I still don't understand."

"That's all right. I don't blame you. Yes, this must sound very confusing. Let me put it another way: The ornament not only grants wishes, it knows ahead of time, every wish that will ever be made. Therefore, to grant *your* wish, to make me know about the power of the charm, the ornament had to first draw me to itself."

"You mean the ornament was making my wish come true before I even wished it?"

"It is something like that. Yes. It at least laid the groundwork."

"But Aunt Loureen, what about the way you celebrate Christmas all winter long? That almost sounds like the people in Lumas."

She smiled. "A mystery, Nephew. That could just be a coincidence or there may be more to it. I really can't say."

"Do you think maybe the ornament found you 'cause you liked Christmas and all?"

"Many people like Christmas."

"But you like it in a special way, Aunt Loureen, kind of like the people of Lumas."

"It is certainly possible, Nephew, and it does my heart good to see you imagining these kinds of wonderful things. We do know the ornament drew me because it anticipated your wish, but yes, if I were not such a fanatic about Christmas, we would never have even had the conversation which encouraged your wish. So it may very well be that the ornament had other motives for selecting me."

❄ ❄ ❄

When the rest of my family got home, they were surprised to see Aunt Loureen. Shelly was very excited. She seemed to remember Sonny's promise that Aunt Loureen would soon return. Mom was hard to figure out. I really don't know how she felt but she was polite as always. Dad looked concerned. He knew that whenever his sister came around, something was up.

Later on, after everyone else went to bed, Dad and Loureen stayed up talking by the fireplace. At first I heard them from my room. Then I snuck down the hall and stayed out of sight so I could hear better.

"So," Dad said. "When are you going to let me in on your little secret?"

"Excuse me?"

"Well I know you weren't just passing through town. And nobody from our family is in the hospital. And it isn't Christmas. What's up?"

"Do I actually need a reason to see my brother and his family?"

"Ah...Just a social call, eh? Even though you were just here, you missed us so much you decided to hop in your car and drive right back."

"Not exactly."

"I didn't think so...I'm waiting."

"You know, James, I remember last summer taking a walk on the beach."

"Oh great! Another story! Spare me, will you? Just skip the details and get to the..."

"Sit down and listen, you pigheaded mule!"

I had never heard Aunt Loureen yell so loud. But Dad *did* quiet down. I guess after all these years he still looked up to her as his big sister. But he also sounded annoyed. "Fine. Go on. You were at the beach and..."

"I saw a family there, two parents and two kids. The little ones were only about four and five years old. I watched them arrive and set up. Mom was frantically rubbing sun tan oil on everybody. Dad was putting up the umbrella as if he had the most important job in the world. But would you like to know what

127

the children were doing?"

"I can't wait."

"They were running around laughing and shrieking with delight, fascinated by everything they saw; not just the waves, but the shells, the seaweed, even the feel of the sand. And when a gull came by begging for food, they got so excited, you'd think the circus was in town. I know how ordinary this all sounds to you, James, but it had a strange effect on me. I tried to remember what it was like to be excited by a piece of seaweed or warm sand running through my fingertips. I thought about how kids are entertained wherever they go. It doesn't have to be a beach. They get excited by grocery store carts, buses, colored Band-Aids, so many things we forget as adults. We forget that life is filled with wonder. I think children know more than we do. I think they intuitively know that life is an incredible experience. Adults don't know that. Adults know work and appointments and schedules and politics and taxes."

"Loureen, this little story moves me close to tears. Now, are you going tell me what's going on?"

"I came to talk some sense into you. I came to save your cat's life."

"The cat? The cat? You drove three-hundred miles for that stupid cat? Where do you come off...?"

"Your family is very upset right now. They're going along with this only because they're too scared to say anything."

"Oh, for crying out loud!" Dad hopped out of his chair and stood in front of the fire. Aunt Loureen got up too, but Dad kept his back to her.

"The cat is a part of the family," she said.

"Part of the family? That flea bitten...? Look, I'm sorry you drove so far. You might just as well have saved yourself a trip."

"I mean to have it out with you about this, James."

Dad picked up the fire place poker and started moving the wood around. "For once...Just for once, would you mind your own business?"

"It's my family too. The only family I have. And Caligula is a part of it."

Dad turned around. "That is such sentimental hogwash. You want to know something about this cat? He's a pill! That's all! A pill! He's stubborn and finicky!"

"So are you. But nobody's putting *you* to sleep."

"Cute, Loureen! Real cute! I'm telling you, I'm fed up. First he wants in. Then he wants out. Then he wants in. Then he's hungry but the food in his dish isn't good enough. He wants some gourmet, fancy feast dinner or whatever they call that tripe on those bonehead cat food commercials."

"Yes. And he scratches up the furniture too. Poor James...Scratched up furniture. How terrible that must be for you."

"Furniture is expensive, Loureen."

"Of course it is. But it's no reason to have him killed."

"I'm not having him killed. I gave him to the pound. If nobody else wants him...Well, tough luck."

"There was a time when the life of a cat meant more to you, back when you were little."

"What are you talking about? We never even owned a cat."

"You had a cat once, a cat that you were close to, a cat who had a strong personality. And you would never have dreamed of putting him to sleep."

"Loureen...Have you flipped? I really have no idea what you're talking about. The cat is gone now and that's all there is to it."

"James!"

"I said that's enough!"

He stormed out of the room, so I ran back fast to my own room. Ten minutes later, I snuck out again and made it into the living room. Aunt Loureen was still sitting by the fireplace.

She didn't even look up at me, but she knew I was there. "Fire is so all compelling, isn't it, Nephew?"

"Yeah. Sorry Dad yelled at you."

"He wasn't always like that."

"I know. He told me."

"He told you what?"

"He told me he was adopted."

Loureen leaned closer. "Told you that, did he?"

"Yeah. I guess that's why he yells so much."

"Nephew, one must never use his past as an excuse. One must always take responsibility for his actions. I know a lot of people who were adopted, and they don't have tempers like your father."

"But it must have been rough on him."

"Yes. It was rough, but he was also given a lot of love by new parents. I know. I was there."

"Do you remember the day Grandma and Grandpa brought him home?"

"Actually, Nephew...I brought him home."

"*You* did?"

"I was at the park with some friends. We happened to notice a little 12 year old boy sitting by himself, under a tree, trying hard not to cry. But we could see how upset he was. He didn't do a good job of hiding it."

"Why was he crying? Because he was lost?"

"Oh, more than lost. Far more. You've heard of the word *amnesia*?"

"Yeah sure. Like when a person loses his memory."

"That's right."

"I saw it once on TV. So, Dad didn't remember who he was?"

"Nobody knew, even after we called the police. They couldn't locate his family anywhere. His first twelve years were a complete blank...until today."

"Huh?"

"Think, Nephew. It was a lost twelve year old boy. Do you know of a lost twelve year old boy?"

All of a sudden it hit me like a ton of bricks. "Sonny! He's twelve! And he was just sent away somewhere! So he's lost, right?"

Aunt Loureen nodded.

"But how could that have been him? That was a long time ago."

"Because angels have special abilities. They can even send people through time. Listen carefully. When Sonny disappeared, he didn't die. Char sent him back through time and took his memory away. Char sent the boy to me. Not the present me, the me in the past, the me who lived as a little girl. I became Sonny's sister. Sonny grew up and became your father."

❄ ❄ ❄

I won't spend a lot of time telling you how weird this all made me feel, 'cause I'm sure you have a pretty good idea already. For hours, Aunt Loureen spoke to me about time travel. She even said that when the ornament knew ahead of time what I would wish for, it was because the ornament could "see all of time in a glance." I told her I didn't know what "seeing time in a glance" meant so she explained some more and tried to make it simple for a kid to understand, but I really didn't understand any of it. The only part I could even follow was the stuff about Dad as a little kid. Finally, she saw how confused I looked and said, "Well, never mind all of that. You'll understand the nature of time and space a few years from now when you start studying physics in high school. For now, the only important thing to grasp is that God can do anything He wants, including sending a person back through time if He so chooses. And God gives some of this power to angels, so they also can send people back through time."

That made more sense. Sure! Char had sent Sonny back through time! That had been the first thing she told me anyway, and I would have understood it fine if she hadn't thrown in all the physics and stuff. But now she boiled it down to just one fact: *Char sent Sonny back through time.* I got it. Not that Aunt Loureen was able to explain *how* he did it. I just mean that with everything else the angels in the ornament had done, it was easier for me to believe in time travel as one more answered wish, instead of trying to understand statements like "all of time in a glance."

After we got the time travel stuff straightened out, Aunt Loureen continued talking about what happened the day she met Sonny in the past. "My girlfriend's mother was a social worker. She took to him immediately and arranged fake papers. Otherwise, without a legal identity, Sonny would have been in foster care the rest of his life. But with fake papers, my parents were able to adopt him. As part of his new, false identity, we gave him the name *James*."

"Did his memory ever come back?"

"Don't you already know the answer to that? Does your dad seem to have a clue? Is he aware of what's going on with the ornament? Does he talk as though he shares your memories?"

"No. But it just seems kind of crazy that he would never remember stuff."

"Well, he did remember one thing, one thing only. He remembered that he was a very mature boy for his age."

"Really? Wow...I guess that figures."

"Even as he got older, James always tried to do the mature thing. That's why he turned out to be so stuffy and unhappy. He'd grown up too fast, never had a chance to be a child."

"Will he ever remember?"

"That's obviously not the intention of the ornament. But I say it's for the best. After all, life would be too bizarre if you and your father shared the same memories. However, we are about to see something better happen. Your dad will soon start remembering, not the events themselves, but the feelings that accompanied the events."

"What do you mean?"

"I mean there's still a child in him who wants to get out and enjoy life as a child."

"Dad's gonna turn back into Sonny again?"

"No. Not like that. He'll remain an adult, but he'll be able to enjoy life again, the only way adults can, by letting the child inside surface from time to time."

"How do you know this will happen, Aunt Loureen?"

"Well, you're the one who wished that I would understand the ornament's power. It seems that wish has been granted progressively, one stage at a time. And what I understand right now is that Char the angel wanted to separate himself from the evil Hamartio. But angels can't do things for themselves, only for others. Char knew that by helping you, he would be pleasing God and then maybe, some day, God would be pleased enough to help him. But it was only a maybe because one should never do favors while expecting something in return."

"How did Char help me?"

"He saw how frustrated you were sharing your life with Sonny. You didn't want Sonny to be you. And actually he never was, I mean, not precisely. He was a duplicate, a copy."

"But Sonny kept saying he was *me*."

"He was created to feel that way. Char…or more correctly put, the part of the ornament's personality which had once been Char, but let's just call him Char…Char gave Sonny your memories so that his life would have some context. He was also made an exact replica to satisfy that wish about sending the ornament home ahead of you. Now, he did come from you and the two of you were certainly linked together. You existed first. You were the true Mike Owen, but Sonny, as a perfect copy, was also you in a very technical sense. And you didn't want him to be you. Char understood that, because, he too, had his identity tied in with another. So Char created a series of steps to separate you. He started by making Sonny a little more mature. Then, as the days went by, Sonny's personality was less and less like yours. Surely you noticed that. Finally Sonny went back through time. When you wished that he would go away, Hamartio could have sent him someplace horrible. That would have been the bad thing for Sonny and the good thing for you, since it was your wish. But Char stepped in instead. He sent Sonny away and in doing so avoided a catastrophe. Sonny still experienced the bad thing of losing his memory but that is nothing compared to what Hamartio would have tried to do. As a result of Char's intervention, he was sent back in time, completely forgetting his original identity and receiving the new name of *James Owen*. This made your dad a distinct person, albeit an unhappy person. And soon now, Char will change that as well by enabling James to be happy again."

"But it's strange, Aunt Loureen."

"Yes?"

"Well...I just mean...Sonny came from me...Then he grew up and..."

"Then he grew up to become your father. Which means you also came from him."

"So, then, are me and Dad really the same person?"

"No. Of course not. But in a way, it is *like that*."

Aunt Loureen could see that I was feeling a little frightened and clueless. "Come here, Nephew. Sit with me. Now then, why the long face?"

"Sometimes I wish I just had a normal life again, like the way things were before all this magic came along."

"The magic was meant to come along. It was destiny. Your life is completely tied to it. And yet, life is still reasonably normal despite the magic. Think, Nephew! Isn't this the way it is with fathers and sons everywhere? On one hand, a son is a continuation of his father. In other ways, he's a completely different person. As human beings we are all connected and we all have the same Creator."

"Dad did say something about me being a part of him since I was his kid and all."

"Yes. And that sounded perfectly normal to you, didn't it? Many fathers say that to their sons, and your dad knew nothing about his history with the ornament when he said it."

"I guess. But it was still strange the way he said it. It was right after he brought me home from the principal's office. He went on and on about how he wanted my life to be better than his. And that was the exact time he told me he'd been adopted."

"I see."

"I always thought it was unusual that he told me right then. And that night, when he overheard me talking to Sonny and came into my room, I lied and said I was listening to the radio, but he looked at me very strange."

"Not so strange. You've heard of the term déjà vu?"

This was the second definition of the evening. First, *amnesia*, now *déjà vu*. I usually didn't like it when Aunt Loureen acted like she was giving me a quiz in one of her classrooms. But I guess it was OK this time, 'cause we were talking about something I really did wanna figure out.

"Yeah...I think...Is déjà vu where you feel like you're seeing something you saw before?"

"Yes, or hearing something you heard before or feeling something you felt before. When your dad looked in the room, it was as though a strange chord was touched way in the back of his heart and mind. Remember, he was already in your room. He was there as Sonny under the bed. He didn't recall the incident exactly, but it gave him a strange sensation. The events of the day sounded familiar to your father but he couldn't remember. Then, all the feelings which went with the events flooded back to the surface. They've been back to the surface ever since. That's why my talk with him went so well just now."

"I don't think it went so well."

"Just wait. Your dad gave his quick, stubborn response. But he still has to sleep at night, and he has many feelings to deal with. You brought them out of hiding. I stirred them up a little. But they're back to stay."

I shrugged my shoulders. "I know things will be OK if you say so, Aunt Loureen. But these last couple of weeks have been real weird."

"Magic can be that way. But life is still life, and when all is said and done, you are still a very normal boy. You are still the same Mike Owen."

Well anyway, it happened just like Aunt Loureen said. Those "familiar feelings" must have been working in Dad all night, because when he woke up in the morning he decided not to go to work, and he hardly said a word during breakfast. Even when Shelly spilled her orange juice, he didn't yell or anything.

After breakfast, Dad grabbed his car keys and took off without telling anyone where he was going. When he got back, Caligula was with him, locked in one of those portable cat carriers. Shelly screamed with delight and ran to let him out of his cage. Mom broke down crying and slobbered Dad with kisses. Then she turned to Shelly. "Let's go. He needs a bath. I'll write you a note and you can go to school a little later today."

"Bath?" Caligula said. "Oh Lord! As if I haven't been through enough already! I'm quite capable of bathing myself, thank you! What do you think goes on when I clean myself? You think I go through that song and dance because I'm fond of hairballs?"

I was the only one who heard him. I guess cats are never satisfied, even when their lives have been saved.

Dad and Loureen were the only ones left in the room with me. At first the just stared at each other for a few seconds.

"I'm proud of you, Brother. You did the right thing."

"I suppose. Somehow I just felt...I don't know...I don't know how I felt."

I thought I saw a tear in Dad's eye. "Hey, big sister, can I have a hug?"

❄ ❄ ❄

Things were different in my family after that. Mom and Dad were happier than I had ever seen them. And I felt like I understood my dad better since I had known him as a boy. I used to wonder what he'd been like as a boy. Every kid wonders that about his father. And I got to actually see it for myself.

Aunt Loureen had a special talk with Shelly. She knew Shelly was too young to understand that Sonny and Dad were actually the same person, so Aunt Loureen made up some story about how Sonny had to go away but would come back some day. She said I could tell Shelly the truth when she was older and could understand better. I tried to be a little nicer to Shelly since she had liked Sonny better than me. I tried to be a better brother. I'm not sure how well I did. My adventures with the ornament had taught me that I wasn't as good a person as I thought. It made me want to be more like my friend Ben. I don't know if I ever will be, but it seems to me that Ben is the kind of person that we should all try to be like.

Oh yeah. You're probably wondering about Renee. Renee did end up moving. I wasn't ever able to tell her how I felt about her. Sonny had been right about that. The night before her last day at school, I cried in my room. Mom and Dad came in and asked if there was anything we needed to talk about. I said, "No."

The next day at school, after class was over, Renee walked up to me in the hallway and handed me a slip of paper.

"That's my new address," she said. "Well, not my real address. It's my grandmother's. We'll be staying there while the Navy helps my dad find a new house. If you like, you can write me."

"Ah...Yeah...Sure...I'll write you, Renee."

I could tell she wanted me to say more. It looked like she wanted to say some stuff too, but we were both shy, and it wasn't gonna happen. I stood in the hallway, watching her walk off with her girlfriends. Once she turned around to see if I was still there. That's the way I'll always remember her, looking back at me one last time. I just hated myself for being such a coward. I guess someday I won't be as scared of girls. But I also know that I'll never again love a girl the way I loved Renee.

I did try to wish for her not to move, but it was no use. Rules are rules, and once the ornament grants a wish, it can't be changed. But even if it could, I actually wasn't able to make any wishes at all anymore because the ornament finally stopped working. All the Christmas lights were gone now, even from the house of the friendly old lady. But at least our family was much happier. The ornament had blessed us just like Aunt Loureen promised.

I even made my peace with Caligula. Aunt Loureen said I should forgive him and not stay mad at him because "after all, he was only a cat." We talked it all out late one night, and I promised to quit bugging him so much.

"I won't ask you questions anymore. I won't make you talk against your will."

For the first time in weeks, I could hear Caligula purring, and his voice sounded gentle. "I appreciate that. Thank you."

"Is it OK if I still pet you once in a while?"

"Of course you can pet me. And maybe scratch me under the chin. I *do* enjoy that...Oh...But only if I'm in the mood. Understand?"

"Yeah, sure."

"You know? You're not so bad for a pugsly little kid. And you've grown through this chain of events. Who knows? Maybe we'll talk again some day."

"Really? You'd be willing to do that? Voluntarily?"

"Why not? I may just be up for it ten years from now, perhaps fifteen."

Aunt Loureen said I should write a book about my adventures with the ornament. I had never written much before. I hated writing essays at school. But I was so excited by the book *The Magic Ornament* that I learned to copy some of its style into my own writing, except without the big words. I don't like big words. I put the big words in only when I was quoting adults or some magic words from the ornament.

Before I started writing, I found myself wondering if the story was really over, so I asked Aunt Loureen if the ornament would work again next Christmas.

"Of course it will," she said.

"But I guess I shouldn't try using it again. I got in so much trouble."

"True. But you'll be a year older next time."

"What about Char? Will he ever be separated from Hamartio? Will he ever get to go back to heaven? And what will happen to the ornament if he does?"

Aunt Loureen gave me a wink. "Other adventures for another time."

I could tell by the sly look on her face that much more was gonna happen with the ornament, maybe not for a while, but it was gonna happen for sure.

Aunt Loureen had gone back home for the second time. Our family was sitting around the fireplace playing a card game. I don't think we had ever played as a whole family without Aunt Loureen before. It made me miss Christmastime. But I was still glad we were playing.

"I can't wait till it's December again," I said.

"Why December?" Dad asked.

"You know…Christmastime."

"Who says Christmas starts in December? I would place the beginning more in November sometime."

"How come? When do *you* think Christmas starts, Dad?"

"When do I think Christmas starts?" he smiled. "When the first light goes up on the first house."

If you enjoyed *The Dangerous Christmas Ornament,* be sure to read the story's next two continuations: *Inside the Castle in the Glass* and *Characters and Kings.*

Made in the USA
Las Vegas, NV
16 December 2023

83016523R00085